Ste

BLOOD IN THE HUERTGEN WOODS

A WWII ACTION NOVEL

EK-2 PUBLISHING

Your Satisfaction Is Our Goal!

Dear Readers,

First, we would like to thank you for purchasing this book. Our goal is to inspire readers from all over the world with our historical and military novels and biographies.

We are a family business, and our team thrives to offer you a unique reading experience and of course, we want to increase our quality with each book published.

We are grateful for your feedback as well as ideas about books you may want to read in the future. Your opinion matters to us. Do you have any comments or criticism? Please let us know. Your feedback is of great value to us and of course to our authors as well. Be part of our publishing journey and our EK-2 publishing family. Write to us at:

info@ek2-publishing.com

And now we wish you an entertaining reading experience with this book.

Your EK-2 Publishing Team
The publisher close to its readers

"The character of a nation is known by the way it treats its soldiers after a lost war."

Leopold von Ranke

Hürtgen Forest, at the Turn of the Year 1944/45

The night lay over Europe. Deep black and silent. Midnight was over.

The American patrol was located in a valley west of Nideggen. First Lieutenant Frederic Miller gazed into the darkness with his night glasses. He had been watching the seemingly endless woods for quite some time. Miller, whom his friends called 'Freddy', lifted his head and listened intently to where the Germans were lying.

Next to the Lieutenant, Sergeant James Clark also listened into the night.

"The darned silence is worse than the fucking German artillery."

And really, it was dead quiet. The deep silence of the night had settled over the forest. At least for the moment. No war cries. No clash of arms. No clattering of entrenchment tools. No sound of the enemy at all.

Miller let the glasses sink and laughed softly: "Don't jinx it, Sergeant. Let us enjoy it as long as it lasts."

They sneaked back to the rest of the squad.

"Coffee, sir?" Radio operator Mellish asked and handed Miller a steaming cup.

"I'd love some. Thank you." Miller gently sipped the steaming cup and then closed his gloved fingers tightly around it.

Copeland, the gunner of the Browing Automatic Rifle or BAR for short, also handed the sergeant a steaming cup. His fellow Wassen, who carried additional magazines for the light machine gun, operated the small stove. Most of the others squatted under the tent tarpaulins and also had their hands around warm cups. They all belonged to the 22nd regiment of the 28th US Infantry Division Keystone.

Suddenly two shots were fired. Scared, the men jumped.

"Holy shit! What the hell was that?" Wassen shouted.

"That sounded like gunfire. It came from our direction and very close by," Clark said with a knowing look.

5

"Take a look, Sergeant," Miller ordered. "Take Copeland, Wassen and Pellosi with you."

"Roger, sir. Come on, men, let's go!"

The soldiers reached for their weapons before they carefully stalked through the bushes towards the source of the noise. A few moments later, Miller heard some angry words. Soon after, the four men reappeared with an fuming look on their faces.

"What was it, Sergeant?" Miller wanted to know.

"That damn war correspondent they assigned us has killed one of the captured Krauts," Clark replied indignantly. "Talked something about trying to escape.

Sir, this isn't the first time this oddball has taken a prisoner aside and then shot him. We should get rid of this guy as soon as possible!"

"I'll do my best, Sergeant." Miller angrily pressed his lips together. The divisional war correspondent should concentrate on his duties instead of running amok! That was madness. But what wasn't in this brutal and inhuman war?

"Better sooner than later, sir," Pellosi said. "He'll wake up the Germans with that noise and then their goddamn artillery will get all over us again."

Pellosi had a point. Miller shook his head.

Then lightning flashed in the East. But unlike a thunderstorm, the lightning did not flash from the sky down to earth, but illuminated the dark horizon in the staccato light of German guns. For a split second the dense snow clouds in the December sky were wrapped in a ghostly glow.

"Madonna, I knew it!" Pellosi cried. "Now we'll get all the blessings!"

"Take cover!" First Lieutenant Miller shouted. He and the men jumped into the painstakingly dug foxholes. Then an inferno of fire, steel, death and destruction swept over the American soldiers.

Miller protected his head with his arms and cursed the war correspondent who had given them the barrage. Goddamn stupid guy, this Hemingway...

*

6

Less than a kilometer away, in Schmidt, German soldiers squatted in badly shot-up buildings. The places near the warm ovens were particularly sought after. In order to avoid tensions, a kind of shift system had been introduced in which everyone could sit near the oven and warm up properly. Fortunately, the population living here had already been evacuated before the first fighting broke out, they would have suffered even worse in the cold. Other soldiers cowered in the corners and slept. They were exhausted.

And the battalion?

How many of them were left?

Loss after loss! The enemy units opposite them had also been decimated, but what did that mean? When one American unit was crushed, two new ones appeared the next moment.

A major sat at the table, on which were some maps and papers. In front of him, on the empty ammunition box, a First Lieutenant was lounging.

"I'd like to welcome you to our troop, Oberleutnant Drechsler," Major Wolfgang Stüttgen said with a hint of a smile on his hardened face. "But I don't think that would be quite reasonable after three months in military hospital."

First Lieutenant Josef Drechsler returned the faint smile, but said nothing. His Knight's Cross shook with every movement of his head.

The major leafed through the marching orders of the newcomer. "You fought as a non-commissioned officer in North Africa, then attended officer's training course and finally took part as a Leutnant in the Normandy theater. ...where you got severely wounded."

The roar of heavy guns interrupted the battalion commander for a short time. The German artillery once again directed harassing fire against American positions.

"I'm assigning you to 2nd Company," the major raised his voice over the roar. "The 2nd has lost almost all its officers and NCOs. A number of men were promoted to fill in the most serious gaps. Experienced personnel are hardly ever sent to the front lines these days ... you're the pleasant exception."

"I understand, Herr Major. What is the strength of the 2nd Company?"

"Strength?" There were wrinkles on Stüttgen's forehead. "Almost the same as the rest of the battalion, about a third of losses of all kinds."

The door opened and a completely filthy soldier entered.

"Shut the fucking door, man!" One of the landsers grumbled at the new arrival. "It's freezing cold out there!"

"You don't have to tell me, comrade," the soldier replied, pulled the scarf from his stubbly bearded face, closed the door and stamped his feet. Snow and mud came off his boots.

"After I pissed, I had to cut off the frozen stream."

"Well, as long as nothing else was damaged," the other sneered with a broad grin on his sunken face.

"Is that you, Rauterkus?" Major Stüttgen shouted.

"Jawohl, Herr Major."

"That's good. Come over here, Unteroffizier. Your new company commander has arrived."

The addressed man hurried over and observed the lieutenant briefly before he saluted him. He did it with his hand on his cap, not with his arm stretched out, as Drechsler noticed. The major made a casual hand movement towards the forehead, which could be a salute or not.

"Rauterkus, this is Oberleutnant Drechsler, the new commander of the 2nd company," Stüttgen announced.

"Willkommen, Herr Oberleutnant," Rauterkus said to Drechsler.

"Unteroffizier."

The two men shook hands.

"If it's all right with you, Major, I would like to join my company as soon as possible."

"Of course." Stüttgen nodded in agreement.

Drechsler imitated the sergeant's military salute, and the major reacted again with his vague hand gesture.

The first lieutenant followed Rauterkus, who opened the door for him and stepped into the cold with his new company commander.

8

"Follow me," Rauterkus said and led the first lieutenant along the partially shot-up and bombed-out buildings. "Our bunch lies on the western part of Schmidt."

It was really cold. The air was burning in the nose. The pitch-black sky lay over the land like a coat, only the stars flashed like polished glass. In the distance, grenades exploded with rumbling racket and shots lit up the horizon. They cast sharp shadows between the houses.

Drechsler grabbed the NCO by the sleeve and pulled him into the entrance of a half collapsed building. A beaming smile spread across his face. "Jesus Christ, Karl!"

Ignoring the dirty uniform, he embraced Rauterkus and patted him on the back. "Nobody knew where you had been!"

"Jupp!" Rauterkus returned the hug. "Damn, it's good to see you!"

A little embarrassed about the outburst of emotion, they stepped back and took a quick look around to see if anyone had been watching them. You couldn't be careful enough.

"They said you were killed in Normandy," Drechsler said.

The NCO snorted, pulled a packet of cigarettes out of his pocket and offered one to his comrade. "That's what you dream of. I didn't even get a scratch in Normandy."

"You always were a lucky bastard, Karl." Drechsler took a cigarette from the packet and put it between his lips. Rauterkus took a storm lighter, shielded it with his hand and let the first lieutenant take the first deep puff before lighting his own cigarette.

"American tobacco," Drechsler noted. "Where did you get it?"

"Where I got this, too," Rauterkus replied, tapping his hand on the holster of the pistol at his hip. Drechsler recognized a Colt .45 in the pale light.

"I see." He inhaled the aromatic tobacco with delight. "How have you been?"

"They posted me from one unit to another until I finally ended up here."

"And you were promoted."

Rauterkus shrugged. "It's only because of the heavy losses. With my record in the personnel file, they never would have promoted me otherwise."

The familiar sense of guilt crept up inside Drechsler. "Listen, Karl..."

"Forget it. I've told you a thousand times, Jupp. It is how it is."

The two men stood next to each other for a few minutes and watched the spectacle of light on the horizon, accompanied by an eerie growl.

"Have you heard anything from anyone?" Rauterkus then asked.

"Jürgen remained at sea with his ship. Achim is reported missing on the Eastern Front. And the old farmer Jost was killed by dive bombers in autumn, together with three foreign workers."

"Oh, damn."

Rauterkus looked sadly on the ground and kicked a lump of snow aside. War wasn't picky, it swallowed them all, soldiers, civilians, men, women, children.

"And Sabine?"

"Misses you more every day."

Once again, they fell silent.

"What about Stüttgen?" Drechsler finally asked.

"The Major is still old school, so he's okay so far."

"And our company?"

"The men are exhausted, many are sick. Whatever supplies are coming through wouldn't be enough for a full platoon. It is an advantage that we are completely undermanned," Rauterkus explained cynically.

"So it's the same as everywhere else," the first lieutenant noted. "Anything else?"

"We don't have a company sergeant major at the moment, the last one was hit by artillery. Your deputy is Leutnant Oettinger. He's fresh from the Napola. Watch out for him. He still thinks Adolf pisses lemonade."

Rauterkus stifled a laugh. He had always liked these sharp comments. Others had not so much.

"Got it."

10

"We should move on before we freeze here," Rauterkus said, stamping his feet.

"Good idea."

They threw the cigarette butts in the snow and continued on their way.

A few Days later

On the Eastern horizon a slight glimmer announced the approach of a new day. The stars in the firmament slowly began to fade. The air was frosty and freezing cold, burning in the lungs with every breath.

The German guard breathed out, while sitting in his foxhole watching the sky.

"Today there seems to be no snow," he said.

"Maybe." His comrade rubbed his fingers, which were cold even with his gloves on.

"I'm so sick of these damned night watches! You freeze your balls off out here while our young Goebbels sleeps out back in the warm house!"

"Shut up, will you!" His comrade immediately cut him short. "Have you taken leave of your senses, Voss? If the wrong person hears this, you're fucked, you idiot."

"I'm just saying," Voss said sheepishly. "I trust you."

"Well, you can. But you have to be more careful."

"You're right. But even the new commander has noticed what's up with Oettinger."

"Yes, Drechsler seems to be all right. I heard he was in Africa and Normandy. So he knows his stuff."

"It's nice to have a company commander for a change who knows his stuff, and doesn't order pointless assault runs into enemy machine gun fire."

"There you go again."

"I'm already quiet. Calm down, Richards."

*

In Schmidt the freezing soldiers with red inflamed eyes and stubbly beards crowded around the open fireplaces. The whole night had been very quiet. Only a few artillery shots or machine gun salvos had startled the men.

In his foxhole, Voss found it difficult to keep his eyes open despite the cold. How he would like to be at home with his wife and children now! Would the little ones even recognize him anymore? Thoughts of home dampened his perception, but now he suddenly got attentive, his senses switching back from those of a family man to those of a veteran. A crunching sound hung in the air, followed by a soft growl.

"Richards... Hey, Richards!"

"Man, you'll make the Yanks get to us!" His comrade complained. "What's the matter?"

"Listen."

"Listen to what?" Richards pulled down the scarf he had wrapped around his shoulders up to his ears. "Oh, damn!"

They listened intently into the beginning of the day. The wind carried the sound in varying volume to them. The rattling of the tracks, the dull roaring of the engines was unmistakable for the soldiers. It hummed as if giants of primeval times were hissing. And above it lay a sound as if masses of empty tin cans were thrown onto a pile of cans that was already lying there.

"They're definitely tanks," Richards exclaimed.

Someone jumped into the foxhole between the two guards and startled them.

"How is it?" Sergeant Rauterkus asked.

"Tanks, Unteroffizier," Voss reported. "You can hear them clearly."

"Ja," Rauterkus agreed thoughtfully and grimaced. "I'll set off the alarm. You will keep still until then."

"Alright, Unteroffizier."

Rauterkus jumped out of the hole and hurried back through the snow as fast as he could.

The two soldiers exchanged a quick glance. Rauterkus was a skilled veteran, as shown by his competence and honors. But Lieutenant Oettinger, also disrespectfully referred to as "junior Goebbels" in the company because of his speeches, had it in for the sergeant from day one. The two young soldiers were sure that there was an interesting story behind it. According to their own logic,

13

someone who got Oettinger upset could not be such a bad guy. But for the time being, they had to deal with the American attack.

"Tanks approaching from the West!" Rauterkus ran along between the buildings and alarmed the troops. "Tanks! Tanks!"

The shouting spread quickly through the village.

"Tanks! Alarm!"

For a second, the still dozing soldiers rubbed their sleepy eyes, then the paralyzing tiredness that made the bones so heavy was suddenly blown away. Everywhere German landsers jumped up and grabbed for weapons and equipment. They grasped hand grenades, anti-tank mines and rocket launchers. They ran between the heaps of rubble towards the outskirts of the village until they stopped at a deep ditch.

Meanwhile the noise increased more and more and the men felt the frozen ground vibrating from the treads of the rolling tanks.

German artillery was now firing. Bullets flew whistling over the crouching soldiers. They could not see the hits from their trenches. The shells pounded the earth somewhere in the dense forest in front of them. The guns fired at the few muddy roads that led through the forest.

Two dark spots detached themselves from a group of trees a few hundred yards away and approached across the adjacent snowy meadow.

Voss squinted his eyes together to see what it was all about.

"Scheisse! Those are Sherman tanks!" He pointed to the shadows.

The two soldiers saw the lightning of the muzzle flash of one combat vehicle's main gun, then the shell exploded with a deafening noise. They ducked into their foxholes, splinters and a few chunks of frozen snow rushed over their heads.

Before the American tanks could fire a second salvo, Rauterkus and Private Hesse, a reserve man, jumped into the trench. They dragged a wooden box with them and immediately tore off the lid. Four thin pipes with a mechanical sighting device, each of which was headed by a thick warhead, came to light.

Panzerfausts!

NCO Rauterkus gritted his teeth. Ten, twelve, fourteen American M4 Shermans appeared in his sight. The steely monsters

14

moved ever closer to the German positions. The M4 weighed a good 30 tons, armed with a 75 millimeter cannon and three machine guns, a heavy one of 12.7 millimeter caliber and two 7.62 millimeter MGs.

Enemy artillery entered the battle bombarding German gun positions. Nevertheless, the German fire was well placed. Shells exploded at treetop level and spiked the surroundings with splinters of steel and wood. Approaching US infantry suffered its first visible losses.

Now the two 75 millimeter anti-tank guns hidden in the village opened fire. A AP projectile hit the spot between turret and hull of the first Sherman. The tank exploded bursting apart in a glowing ball of fire, which roared and rose in front of the American tank convoy. A shattering sight, which surely had a devastating effect on the other Sherman crews.

A second tank suddenly turned completely on its own axis before it came to a standstill smoking. One bullet had torn off its left track.

The anti-tank guns fired again and another M4 got a direct hit. The explosion hurled the heavy turret of the combat vehicle up into the air before it crashed onto the snow-covered ground.

Eleven to go, Rauterkus thought to himself.

At full speed the steel beasts raced towards the German positions. The muzzle flashes of their cannons and machine guns flared up continuously. Behind Rauterkus, a half-destroyed house flew apart in a fountain of dirt and fragments, which poured down on the soldiers in their holes. Splinters, bits of ice and frozen earth struck the men on their steel helmets and shoulders.

"That was pretty damn close," Richards growled.

"Yes." Gently, Rauterkus moved his head over the edge of the shelter. The American tanks came closer and closer. Hissing, a projectile roared over his head and crashed down just behind him. A gush of snow fell on Rauterkus, threatening to bury him underneath. Hastily the sergeant knocked large, white chunks off his uniform jacket.

"Two tanks are a bit ahead of the others. We must eliminate them first." The calmness with which the sergeant uttered these words did not at all fit the situation. Both he and Voss took up one Panzerfaust tube each.

If the tanks continued in the same direction, they would roll past along their position. Rauterkus based his attack plan on this.

The powerful engines of the M4 roared very close. The frozen ground vibrated under the advance of the colossuses, first cracks appeared in the walls of the trenches. Earth trickled onto the soldiers crouching at the bottom. Less than five meters to the left and to the right of the hole the first two tanks rumbled past.

"Ready! Fire!"

Two dirty faces were aiming at the back of a Sherman via the sight of their Panzerfausts. They pulled the trigger. The hollow charge warheads raced towards the rear of the tank they were targeting, then the terrible detonation forced the Landsers back into the shelter of their hole. Peering up over the rim, Rauterkus, Richards, Voss and Hesse watched as the turret of the tank shot up on a column of fire.

On their left, triumphant cries of joy were heard. The second M4 over by the first lieutenant's hole was also in bright flames.

"They're done," Rauterkus said.

Hesse and Richards grabbed the two remaining Panzerfausts and jumped up. Ten yards away from the burning tank wreckage at the first lieutenant, a Sherman was rolling and Richards now fired his Panzerfaust, aiming between the road wheels. The warhead pierced the thin, lateral armor protection of the hull and sent a shower of shrapnel through the interior of the M4. Glowing hot pieces of metal, fragments from the penetrated armor as well as from the warhead, tore open fuel lines and tank shells for the main gun. The mixture of a mist of diesel fuel and propellants ignited almost immediately. Flames flared up from all hatches. More ammunition went off with a rattling sound and the Sherman slowly came to a halt.

As Richards dived back into the shelter of his foxhole, a salvo of bullets hit the edge of the trench. American half-tracked vehicles had driven up and fired on the German lines. Hesse collapsed to the ground with a gargling sound. One of the finger-thick bullets had torn open his neck. Bright red blood stained Richards' trousers and boots.

"Shit, the kid's been hit!"

Richards pulled a first aid kit from his pocket and wrestled the wildly flailing Hesse to the ground. He pressed the gauze onto the bloody pond, but his experience told him the wound was too severe.

In front of the German lines, seven enemy tanks were already scattered across the terrain as burning wrecks. The remaining Sherman fired wildly into the surrounding area.

"American infantry!"

These words were enough for the men to let sweat pour out of their pores. The Americans often attacked the German lines with overwhelming firepower and in superior numbers until they finally gave in or were broken through. Usually, in addition to the artillery, the Allied air forces also battered their opponents. But this time at least the Germans were spared enemy aircraft, as they could not make out their targets in the dense woods and the chaos of close-quarter combat that reigned warfare in the Hürtgen Forest. Meanwhile the Germans rarely saw their own planes at all, the Allied air superiority was too strong.

Now the machine guns of the Germans, which had been mute until then, opened fire. The MG42s covered the foreland and had a terrible harvest in the ranks of the Americans.

At the rear, between the ruins of the houses of Schmidt, the mortars of the company opened up. A chain of detonations tore large gaps in the ranks of the US infantry, who rushed towards the German positions like a tidal wave.

"Just in time," Rauterkus said.

In private, Voss thought the same.

The NCO turned to Richards. "What about Hesse?"

Richards shook his head. He picked up a handful of slush from the ground and tried to get the blood off his hands.

"Damn it."

A squad of Americans charged forward and got into the minefield in front of the German lines. Antipersonnel mines detonated. Terrible screams pierced the clamor of the battle.

17

But even this did not stop the American assault. More and more men, half-tracked vehicles and tanks rummaged out of the protection of the forests.

"They want it," Rauterkus muttered, raising his submachine gun. "Aim for them, men!"

He pulled the trigger and distributed short bursts of fire among the attacking enemy.

Richards and Voss fired their rifles 98k as fast as they could load a new cartridge into the chamber. Once again, the Americans' firepower proved superior to their own. The enemy was generously equipped with a variety of automatic rifles and machine guns, while the majority of German troops were still fighting with the same weapons as at the beginning of the war.

Then the shells of the US artillery also rushed in. Guns of all calibers tried to shoot the German lines ripe for attack. The hits were getting closer and closer. Dirt and splinters flew so close to the ears of the soldiers that they literally lost sight and hearing. Every second the dense bombardment ripped new fountains out of the ground. The number of defenders decreased. The moaning of the dying and the groaning of the wounded was drowned in the bursting of the explosions. The hurricane of the enemy's fire drum swept everything away.

Above the roaring a single whistle was heard, producing three short whistles twice – the agreed retreat signal.

"Retreat to the second line," Rauterkus shouted against the infernal noise. "Come on, retreat!"

The men crawled out of their half-buried holes and trenches and fled into the shelter of the buildings of Schmidt. Others had not heard the signal and died in their positions. Bullets and grenades tore further gaps in the ranks of the soldiers. Who was hit and who made it to safety was determined by chance.

*

"They're retreating! Now we've got them," Major Robert Mac-Graw exclaimed enthusiastically. The battalion commander bent over the side armor of his M3 command vehicle as far as he could

18

and watched through the binoculars as the Germans retreated. "They're on the run!"

The American tank crew was now only 200 yards away from Schmidt and rushed through the opening gap in the German defense line.

"Every available man is to advance immediately!"

"This could still be an ambush, sir," one of his staff officers stated.

"Humbug!" MacGraw hissed, angrily glaring at his staff. "The Krauts are turning tail! And I'll be damned, if I let them get away now, so they can regroup later! Advance!"

Schmidt was just a prize the divisional general was determined to win, and the commander who served it to him on a silver platter would be in his favor. MacGraw intended to be that man.

His staff officers had not been unaware of their superior's ambitions. There was some doubt as to the boldness of MacGraw's strategy. The Germans fought for every lump of earth like wolves defending their cubs, only retreating when it was unavoidable, using every opportunity to counter-attack, thus literally bleeding the attacking Allied units dry. Mobile warfare could only be achieved by dearly bought frontal attacks that tore a hole in the enemy lines – the Allies in Normandy had succeeded in this – but in this area, the Wehrmacht and the impassable terrain had prevented such an approach so far. The Germans also fought from well protected positions and decimated every wave of attack. Air raids on targets behind the German lines weakened their front units, but still did not bring the desired breakthrough. It was understandable that an ambitious man like MacGraw wanted to force that very breakthrough. The Germans were badly hit, somewhere their lines finally had to give way, so why not here?

His the staff relayed the orders and the American troops rushed into the gap towards Schmidt.

*

First Lieutenant Miller and his platoon were among the first Americans to enter the town. There was confusion; there was no time for a coordinated approach.

19

"This is a very bad idea, Lieutenant," Sergeant Clark growled at his platoon leader as they passed the first buildings under cover of some tanks and half-track vehicles.

"We'll do what we're ordered to do, Sergeant."

"Yes, sir." Clark bent his head to one side and heard German artillery gun shells howling despite the noise of the engines. He dragged Miller with him and jumped into a German foxhole. A dead Kraut lay there in his blood, his body torn apart by explosions.

They ducked their heads and there was a deafening crash. Small stones and earth rained down on their helmets and shoulders. The sergeant peered out of the hole and saw that three half-track vehicles were on fire. A dozen men were dead, many more wounded.

Combat medic Burns advanced very quickly, paying little attention to the enemy shells that were falling down from the sky in large numbers. Burns immediately rolled a GI on his back for medical attention.

"Oh, damn it, sir! That's Mitchum!" Clark shouted and jumped out of the hole.

"Clark, damn it," Miller yelled and followed his sergeant, who rushed to the wounded man.

A new cluster of enemy shells howled closer.

"Give me a hand, Sarge!" The medic demanded. Together they dragged Mitchum into a half collapsed building. There was a rumble, and the dilapidated building shook under the impact of the German artillery. Dust trickled down from the walls.

Mitchum had pressed his hands onto a large stomach wound, blood gushing out between his fingers, and he groaned appallingly. Burns only needed a quick look at the ghastly wound to see that there wasn't much he could do. He injected Mitchum with morphine to at least take away the worst of the pain.

"Sarge?" Mitchum moaned.

"Take it easy, son. You'll be all right," Clark assured him.

Mitchum trembled. "Sarge?

"What is it?

Mitchum struggled to say more words as life slipped away from his ravaged body. Clark had to bend over to understand him.

"Why?" Mitchum whispered.

What was the answer to that question? How could a soldier even ask it?

Mitchum seemed to stare through the shattered roof into the cloudy sky. He had stopped breathing. With thumb and forefinger, Clark closed the soldier's broken eyes. Deep melancholy came over him. He had little to do with this boy, but it seemed unfair that the young private had to die.

"We have to keep moving, sergeant," Miller softly reminded him.

"Yes, sir. I'm coming."

*

Under Rauterkus' command, four soldiers fired their Panzerfausts and scored three hits against the American tanks rolling up the main road. Sparks rained down from two Shermans, the tracks came to a standstill, the turrets stopped moving. When a hatch flew open, Rauterkus saw dazzling white flames shooting out. A tank driver who was on fire was hitting his clothes as he rolled off the Sherman and finally lay on the road.

Behind the burning tanks other Shermans were already approaching.

"Everybody cover!" Rauterkus yelled, while throwing himself down. His MP40 hit painfully against his right side. The next moment several shots from tank guns shook the road. Shrapnel blasted into the house where the sergeant's men had sought shelter. Debris shattered through clouds of dust and smoke, plaster trickled from the walls and ceiling. In the distance the shrill cry of a wounded man was heard.

"Stay down!" Rauterkus shouted against the chaos.

Further projectiles of all calibers hit the brick wall of the house. The ground vibrated. Terrible screams were ringing through the house. In Rauterkus' back the living room exploded. Flames hissing through the air caused serious burns.

Rauterkus could no longer breathe. He didn't know whether he was dead or alive. He rolled over on his stomach and pushed his upper body up.

21

Voss and Richards lay moaning beside him. They didn't seem to be wounded, just dazed. Two other comrades in the living room had been less lucky, their bodies had been torn to pieces. Outside, an MG42 was hammering away at the enemy.

Rauterkus moaned as he pulled himself to his knees on the window frame. Through the smoldering frame he had a perfect view of the hell that had opened up around him.

Just 15 yards away, a Yank knelt and shot down the street with his BAR. Rauterkus put the MP40 against his shoulder and fired a salvo that knocked the enemy soldier to the ground. But the latter, completely unexpectedly, staggered up again. Rauterkus had to finally knock him down with another fire burst.

Machine guns rattled; rifles popped. The other surviving defenders now demanded the price the Americans had to pay if they wanted to conquer this street.

Richards pulled himself up and glanced briefly into the living room – he wished he hadn't done it. He had to gag, almost threw up. He pulled himself together, broke off the lower part of each dog tag and took them.

Meanwhile three tanks stood on the road as burning wrecks, no vehicle could get past them.

But now American infantrymen appeared on the street. Always looking for cover, they worked their way up the road in groups. They passed brightly burning Sherman tanks, in which corpses were roasting.

"Richards! Voss! Get back! Come on."

Rauterkus had inserted a full magazine into his submachine gun and immediately emptied it into the ranks of the attackers. Under his cover, Richards and Voss were able to grab their weapons and disappear through the kitchen and out the back door.

Outside, hundreds of projectiles whistled through the streets, finding targets again and again among the soldiers on both sides.

While Rauterkus fired his MP40, he hardly noticed the enemy bullets anymore. Projectiles darted through the open window and hit the wall behind him. His submachine gun's barrel rested on the windowsill, it repeatedly spewed short bullet salvos. After he had used up his remaining ammunition and the weapon ticked like a hot tea kettle, the NCO lowered it and pulled an egg-shaped grenade from his belt instead. But even before he could pull the pin, Rauterkus saw the Americans in turn hurling several grenades in his direction.

Oh shit!, the NCO thought and threw himself to one side. The walls, the roof and the garden brightened up in fiery flashes of light and the room from which they had put up such fierce resistance was suddenly ablaze.

Time to leave!

Rauterkus rushed to the back door, having to bend down low because of the smoldering cross beams in the kitchen. Behind him an HE round exploded in the living room. The shock wave hurled him into the garden behind the house.

"Over here!" Richards yelled and Voss waved. The two soldiers squatted at the end of the garden behind the low wall and fired some last shots from their rifles at the house and the street. They heard English curses and screams from there.

Rauterkus ran as fast as he could. Bullets whirred around his ears. He dashed over the wall and slammed into the slush lengthwise. His lungs burned and he gasped for breath. Sweat was pouring down his dirty face. He ignored his aching body, forced himself up, leaned his back against the wall and tried to catch his breath.

Richards fired one last shot, then his rifle clicked empty. The corporal began frantically searching his ammunition pockets.

"Oh, shit," he moaned. "Anybody got any more rounds?"

"I don't have any more either," Voss replied in a hoarse voice, full of tension.

"Scheisse! Now they're screwing us!"

Rauterkus pulled the captured Colt pistol out of its holster. Now he could at least defend himself.

A bullet smashed against the wall and bounced off.

On the upper floor of the half collapsed neighboring house, an MG42 suddenly opened up and covered the street and the front of the building that had just provided cover for the three soldiers. Two GIs went down howling, the others quickly took cover.

"This is our chance," Rauterkus said. "Come on, retreat!"

The three men jumped up and ran across two adjoining gardens. There they met their company commander, First Lieutenant Drechsler, who was already waiting for them with the meager rest of 2nd Company.

"Are these all of the men, Unteroffizier?" Drechsler shouted over the stapling of the machine gun.

"That's all, Herr Oberleutnant."

Drechsler and Rauterkus changed a grief-stricken look, then nodded to each other and led the men to the next assembly point.

Behind them, the MG42 still barked angrily, as if the gun was taking it personally that it too could not stop the American advance.

*

The air was filled with the howling of the shells and the whirring of the countless bullets that raced through Schmidt. An American M3 half-tracked vehicle stood across the street, its snout had dug into one of the abandoned houses, causing it to collapse. Now the M3 was stuck in the ruins. Bullets smacked against the side armor, ricochet off and hissed away in all directions.

A young soldier cowered behind the M3. His face was as white as chalk, his lips were only a thin line, his eyes were wide with fear.

First Lieutenant Miller felt pity for the young GI. The first combat mission, even under the best of circumstances, was a terrible thing. In this case, the circumstances were anything but favorable. Schmidt formed a deadly trap; the narrow alleys with their buildings hindered the vehicles and offered the Germans an excellent field of fire. Inside the houses there were riflemen with rocket launchers and machine guns.

In the ripped open front of a tavern, muzzle flashes flared up and again a metallic hailstorm hit the hull of the half-track vehicle.

"Sounds like a damn Hitler's Buzzsaw," Sergeant Clark snorted next to Miller.

24

Hitler's Buzzsaw. That's what the GIs called the German MG42. The damn thing fired up to 1,500 shots a minute and could be identified by the typical clatter of its bursts of fire.

"I'd say so, Sarge," the lieutenant agreed. He touched the trembling boy on the shoulder, who then jerked around in horror.

"Hand me one of your grenades, soldier."

"Y-yes, sir," the private stammered and handed Miller one of his grenades.

"Private Copeland?"

"Here, sir!" Copeland, a big, burly lad, carried the heavy BAR. He chewed a few ounces of tobacco with his back teeth.

"On the count of three, you cover Sergeant Clark and me."

"Roger, sir."

"Clark, ready?"

"Ready, sir." The Sergeant was already holding his own grenade.

"Attention, Copeland! One, two, three. Now!"

Copeland shot with his light machine gun from the hip. Around the enemy position mortar and stone splinters burst from the walls. Some bullets pierced the wall, punching holes in it. For a second, the German machine gun fire stopped.

"Grenade!"

Miller and Clark reached back and tossed the grenades at the machine gun nest. One fell too short and detonated in the rubble just outside the wall, the other landed inside the building and went off. The MG42 fell silent.

Time to earn your extra five dollars a week, Freddy, thought First Lieutenant Miller with a touch of gallows humor.

It took a tremendous effort to leave safe cover and expose oneself to enemy fire. Someone had to lead by example and carry the men along. Miller checked his Thompson submachine gun, took a deep breath and then shouted, "Everybody's going ahead! Follow me!"

He jumped around the rear of the M3 and ran down the road.

"The lieutenant's completely nuts, Sarge," Mellish said.

"Shut up! You heard the man! Let's go! Move!" Clark urged the men on.

25

Copeland had rammed a fresh magazine into his BAR and stormed after Miller. Wessen and Pellosi followed next. Halting the others left their covers. Shots blasted and missed Miller and Copeland, but caught Wessen running in front of Pellosi. A bullet went through his body at chest level and Pellosi saw the blood spurting out the back, before he fell and lay motionless.

Miller reached the building out of which the MG42 had been fired. He took cover behind the pile of rubble that had once formed the front of the building. He could see the barrel of the German machine gun and he felt as if that barrel was moving again. Miller grabbed his Thompson, held it over his head and emptied the magazine into the machine gun nest. A sound of pain was heard over the drumming of the submachine gun. The lieutenant finally put it down, took out another grenade, pulled the pin and hurled the lethal egg inside the building. The detonation shook the whole house.

Now Copeland was there too, firing wildly into the building and throwing himself to the ground on the other side of the pile of rubble.

Pellosi landed beside him, breathing heavily. "How can you run so fast with that heavy piece?"

"Exercise," Copeland promptly returned and inserted a fresh magazine. "Played football in school. Where's Wessen?"

"He's dead."

Copeland spits out some chewing tobacco. "Ah, hell, he owed me two bucks from poker."

"You're a dick, Copeland! What would you have said if they'd killed me?"

"The Krauts aren't shooting at you."

"What's that supposed to mean?"

"Well, you're Italian. They think you're their ally."

"I'm an American," Pellosi shouted angrily and patted himself on the chest. "So fuck you, Copeland!"

"You shouldn't make offers like that to people bigger and stronger than you, kid."

"Are you finished cuddling?" Sergeant Clark shouted. He had thrown himself into the dust next to Mellish and the lieutenant. "You better get a room for this!"

"That'll never happen, Sarge!" Copeland returned.

"We're going in," First Lieutenant Miller announced.

Pellosi grabbed the rosary from under his shirt and kissed it, then he tightened his grip on his M1 rifle.

"Let's go!"

The men jumped up, climbed over the rubble and entered the building. Four Germans were down. Large pools of blood had formed around their bodies.

Copeland turned one of the bent bodies with the tip of his boot, holding the barrel of the BAR pointed at his head. The German was a young lad, not a year older than himself. His lifeless eyes seemed to stare accusingly at Copeland.

"Son of a bitch," the GI muttered in a low voice.

"Secure the building," Miller ordered. "See if there are any more Krauts around."

*

First Lieutenant Drechsler wiped the sweat from his eyes with his sleeve and thus spread the dirt on his face even more. Then he listened to the sounds of the still raging battle in Schmidt.

Rauterkus pulled out a clean handkerchief and held it out to the officer without a word.

Drechsler accepted the offer and thanked the sergeant with a slight nod.

They squatted in a ditch half filled with snow, through which a now completely frozen little stream ran. The outermost houses of Schmidt shielded them from the Americans for the moment. The few soldiers who still had ammunition cowered at the top of the trench and secured it.

"We have to retreat to the third line," Drechsler said after a moment's reflection.

27

"I'm afraid so too, Herr Oberleutnant. The Yanks make a lot of pressure. It seems as if they really want Schmidt," Rauterkus said sarcastically.

Drechsler grinned crookedly. "You'd think so."

"I'm against it!" Lieutenant Oettinger walked up to them. He had followed the fighting from his observation post in the church tower so far and was therefore the only one still reasonably clean.

"We have to get the Americans out of the town as soon as possible!" The Lieutenant exclaimed. "We can't give the enemy even one more meter of ground! We must counterattack immediately!"

"The men have been fighting all day, they are exhausted and don't have much ammunition left. In addition, we mourn heavy losses," Rauterkus said. "We first have to assemble and regroup. By then it will be dark for quite some time."

"The courage and bravery of the German soldier are sufficient to defeat any enemy, even if on paper they are outnumbered three to one," Oettinger intoned.

"But courage and bravery are no substitutes for missing ammunition," Rauterkus returned pointedly. "And beating a Sherman tank with bare fists is not something I consider particularly effective."

Oettinger blushed in anger and clenched his fists. The Lieutenant was just taking a deep breath to shout at the NCO when Drechsler intervened.

"Stop it! We gather at the third line of defense and prepare for the counterattack. I will coordinate our further actions with Major Stüttgen. Leutnant Oettinger, see that the men get new ammunition, some food and a good night's sleep!"

The lieutenant choked down his anger with difficulty. "Jawohl, Herr Oberleutnant!" He snared, standing so stiffly that he shook with tension and greeted with an outstretched arm.

But he had the misfortune to stand on a completely icy part of the little stream. He slipped and landed with flailing arms on his backside.

The men standing behind the lieutenant and thus out of his sight grinned maliciously at this misfortune.

28

"Be careful, Leutnant," Rauterkus said dryly, holding out his hand to Oettinger. "There's ice under the snow."

"Thank you for pointing that out, Unteroffizier," Oettinger snapped and ignored the offered hand. He picked himself up and tried to keep his dignity as best he could.

Drechsler had to bite his cheek in order not to laugh out loud. He let his gaze wander over the smirking men and glared at them angrily.

They understood and immediately started to move.

"Rauterkus, just a moment," Drechsler said and waved the sergeant over to him. The first lieutenant waited until the men were well away before telling the sergeant to follow them. Drechsler also began to walk.

"Tell me, are you crazy?" He wanted to know right away. "Fighting Oettinger in public!"

"That fellow is bugging everybody, you saw that," Rauterkus replied. "He is always talking about how beautiful and honorable it is to die for Führer and Vaterland. Just like he learned it at the Napola. Of course, this only applies as long as it is not his own precious skin that is at stake. He' s above that. But he has no qualms about letting a squad run against a machine gun without any covering fire. The comrades all died!"

Drechsler thought about this while they left Schmidt behind and went to the part of Nideggen still occupied by the Wehrmacht forces.

Oettinger was the product of a Napola, a national-political academy where future leaders were drilled for the Reich.

"Oettinger is one of the true believers," Rauterkus continued. "He was even a leader in the Hitler Youth and is quite proud of it, which is why he wears all those Hitler Youth badges on his chest. Well, he doesn't have any other honors to show!"

"We didn't have people like that in Africa," Drechsler grumbled. Despite all his experiences, it seemed like better times. In North Africa, the British and Germans had fought each other tooth and nail, but had always tried to maintain honor and decency. This was due to their commanders at that time, Rommel and Montgomery, both outstanding personalities in their own way.

29

"Nevertheless, hold yourself back, Karl," Drechsler warned. "Oettinger has it in for you."

"I know."

Everywhere in the destroyed houses wounded people were sitting or lying, who had been injured in the recent battles. They didn't yet have the time to bring everyone back. Some groaned, others rolled back and forth in pain, others suffered silently. Perhaps they had already died. The sight of all the pain and suffering almost tore Drechsler's heart apart. He noticed that Rauterkus felt the same way.

They turned away and went to the command post, which was in the cellar of a house that was almost completely destroyed. Lieutenant Oettinger was already there, giving a lecture to a group of soldiers.

"As soon as the new wonder weapons come to the front, we'll drive the Anglo-Americans back into the sea," he announced confidently.

It was obvious what some of the unwilling listeners thought of such promises.

Drechsler raised his eyebrows. Whenever he thought Oettinger had already reached the limits of what was possible, the lieutenant topped it. He wanted to give Rauterkus a warning look when he saw that the sergeant's crest was already rising.

"Oh really, Leutnant?" Rauterkus hissed. "And when are the wonder weapons to come?"

"That will happen every day now, Unteroffizier," Oettinger said patronizingly.

"Will that help us here in the Eifel too?"

"We'll stop the decadent Yanks," Oettinger replied a bit too hastily, "as soon as our factories have produced enough wonder weapons, we'll finish them off with root and branch."

"Well, then we can only hope that our eggheads will not have to deliver their wonder weapons to the Americans right away, who will soon enough knock on the factory gates in a friendly manner," Rauterkus said with biting sarcasm, causing a broad grin among the soldiers, which the men could hardly hide.

Lieutenant Oettinger's face turned an angry red.

30

"A very accurate statement, Herr Unteroffizier," Major Stüttgen said and smiled slightly. "I am sure that the wonder weapons will be ready in time. Wouldn't you agree with me, Unteroffizier Rauterkus?"

"Of course, Herr Major."

Stüttgen nodded. "Well... Drechsler, a brief report, if you please."

"Immediately, Herr Major. Unteroffizier, check the guards again. We don't want any Yanks to visit us."

"Yes, Herr Oberleutnant." Rauterkus saluted and slipped away. Oettinger narrowed his eyes and gave him a very angry look.

Drechsler followed the major to the back of the cellar. Empty ammunition boxes once again provided a table and seats.

"Unteroffizier Rauterkus takes a lot of liberties," Stüttgen said with a calm voice. "But I can't stay mad at a veteran with his honors for very long."

Stüttgen's eyes looked at the badges that adorned Drechsler's chest.

Rauterkus had been awarded the Iron Cross 1st and 2nd class, as well as the Close Combat Clasp in gold and other honors. First Lieutenant Drechsler wore the same badges and also the Knight's Cross. Stüttgen also wore one on his neck, but his was from the last war.

"Karl always had a big mouth," Drechsler let slip.

The major looked thoughtful. He sat down and pointed to another ammunition box. "Somehow I had the impression that you two were acquainted."

"Ever since we were kids. We only lived a few houses apart and were practically inseparable."

"Let me guess: He followed you to the army, right?"

"No, it's the other way around. I followed him to the army. Karl is two years older than me, and he was in officer's school at the time."

Stüttgen frowned. "Oh? Then why isn't Rauterkus an officer?"

Drechsler writhed uncomfortably on his "chair." His old guilt was back.

"If you don't want to talk about it, I'll understand," Stüttgen said politely. He pulled out an old pipe and stuffed it.

"It' s not that, Herr Major." Drechsler took a deep breath. "Our family runs the village pub in our home town. My sister Sabine also works there. We were all sure she and Karl would get married one day. But then the local party chairman approached her."

"I have a bad feeling." Stüttgen lit his pipe.

"Yes, the gold pheasant was really misbehaving. When he touched my sister, I was about to punch him in his teeth, but Karl stopped me. He asked the party bigwig to keep his hands off Sabine. The gold pheasant just laughed at him and grabbed Sabine's breast. Karl then broke his jaw. In the court of honor, they considered it an attack on the party."

Stüttgen exhaled a cloud of smoke. "Was your so-called gold pheasant in uniform?"

"Sure, but that had nothing to do with it. The guy's always been an ass. Dieter Uhl is his name. He runs a small construction company. Everyone has confirmed what happened, but you know how it is. The bigwigs stick together. That' always been the case and always will be."

The major didn't show whether he really knew this kind of thing.

"Anyway, they threw Karl out of the officer's school and drafted him as a private. Later, we ended up in the same unit and were sent to Africa. There we were both wounded in an air raid at the end of '42 and flown out. After recovery we were sent to Normandy, where he saved my life twice. When I was wounded again, I lost sight of him."

"Until you found him here." Stüttgen sucked on his pipe again. "The Wehrmacht is a village! And Rauterkus is a good man. I wish I had more men like him."

The two officers looked at each other briefly and nodded.

The next Morning

Sergeant Rauterkus had actually been able to get a full five hours of sleep. One quickly learned to enjoy such small comforts. Now he walked along the front line and talked to the soldiers who were anxiously awaiting an attack by the Americans. Rauterkus' eyes finally fell on their last trump card, two Flak 36 8-8s or "Acht-Achts". Until now the flak canons had not yet intervened in the fighting. And the enemy would certainly be impressed once the heavy guns went off. The Germans had learned to rely on the overwhelming firepower of the 8-8. Not only could this gun be used to fight aircrafts, but it also had a devastating effect against ground targets. A group of Flak artillerymen had made this experience when they were attacked by tanks and fired their guns directly at the attackers – with astonishing effects. Since then the 8-8 was to be found everywhere where German soldiers were present. In the region of Drechsler's 2nd company the two 88 millimeter guns controlled the main road in both directions.

Rauterkus continued his patrol. If the low-hanging, dark grey snow clouds had not been there, it would already have been rather bright.

The sergeant stopped. Listened. Tank engines roared up from the direction of Schmidt. Apparently the Americans proceeded differently this time by refraining from any initial artillery fire.

Rauterkus raced off as if stung by an adder and reported: "Alarm! The Yanks are coming!"

"Man, you don't even have time to eat," Voss complained and stuffed his sandwich into his bread bag.

Rauterkus paused when he noticed that the battalion came to life. Now everyone could hear the enemy tanks rolling relentlessly towards their position.

Muffled shouts were heard: "Keep calm now, we have our 8-8, it'll stop the bastards!"

"Do we have any mines left?"

"What do you want with them? They're no use to us now."

"Hand out the Panzerfausts, come on!"

As the first two mud-caked Sherman tanks came up the village street, the soldiers hiding behind house walls and in cellar corners struggled for breath. Fear of death spread and threatened to overwhelm them. They did not even dare to cough any more, although they knew that the five-man tank crew in their steel monster could not even hear loud screams, since they were wrapped up in the roaring of the powerful engine and their ears were closed by bulky headphones. Nevertheless, fear paralyzed the Germans lurking in their hiding places. Trembling forefingers twitched around the triggers.

About 200 yards in front of a partially shot-up residential building, which contained the foremost position of the German defenders, the steely colossus leading the American formation stopped. Its turret with the cannon swung searchingly around. The following Sherman rolled on for half a tank length, then came to a halt as well. It was impossible to tell how many tanks were following them, as the road behind them bent, but judging by the roar and rattle, there must have been at least three.

"Shit, why don't we ever have our own panzers when the enemy's armor is coming out?"

"That would be too easy, wouldn't it, Richards?" Voss replied.

"Put your head down or you'll lose it," Rauterkus hissed.

They waited anxiously in the ruins, wondering what would happen next.

The turret of the first Sherman slowly swung back around. Had the gunner identified a target worth firing at? Or did the commander just want to look around as well as the narrow optics allowed him to?

With a bang that threatened to tear the eardrums, the first HE shell ruptured out of the tank's gun barrel. It went into the ground at least 20 yards to the side of Rauterkus' position. Shrapnel splinters flew over the sergeant and his comrades, dirt and stones rained down on them.

One of the new recruits clasped his thigh and started screaming like crazy: "Ah! My God! I got hit! Ahh!"

Rauterkus leaned over to the wounded man and pulled his knife out of the waist belt. The eyes of the greenhorn widened, his cries became increasingly panicky. "No! No, stay away!"

Richards already pressed the wounded man to the ground, skillfully restraining the arms of the flailing boy, while Rauterkus stuck the sharp point of the knife into the wound. The red-hot shrapnel had to be removed from the leg before it could eat its way into the muscles and bones. The blade dipped into the burnt flesh, dark blood gushing out from under the metal. Rauterkus levered with the tip of the blade until a glowing piece of metal emerged from the blood-red lake. The wounded man screamed his head off, desperately and unsuccessfully fighting against Richards, who fixed him in place. Richards had to use considerable force to restrain him. Rauterkus managed to remove the splinter, burning his fingertips on it.

"Damn."

Lehmann, the medic, injected the young soldier, whose cries subsided slowly. "That'll do it," Lehmann said, dressing the wound.

Rauterkus nodded at him and grabbed a Panzerfaust.

If only there was not this unnerving humming and rattling of the enemy tanks!

The Sherman's roar had a considerable effect on the defenders. The terrible noise could paralyze a man, turning him into a mouse who did not dare to fight a tiger. More and more Sherman drove up the road, followed by infantry advancing under the tank's protection.

The firing of the two 8-8 almost started at the same time. Two Shermans were struck. Their fuel or ammunition supplies seemed to have been hit, as walls of fire and fume ascended from their hulls.

Several of the following tanks hit the stern of the vehicle upfront as their drivers frantically slammed on the brakes. The Americans recognized immediately what they were dealing with. The devastating effect of the 8-8 was also familiar to them.

Once again, the German guns fired. One Sherman had its turret blown off in a fiery blaze, the next had his right track torn off.

35

Immediately the damaged tank turned sideways and blocked the road for the other combat vehicles.

At this moment a MG42 started to deliver barrage fire to trap the American infantrymen who huddled together behind the remaining Shermans.

Another tank went up in flames. The crew got out and ran for their lives. Spraying fountains of earth marked their way. One of the tank men bent his back, seemed to reach for the sky for a moment, and then fell.

Two more tanks fell victim to the 8-8 on the broad road, then the first Sherman managed to pull back. The others followed after it, back into the shelter of the houses of Schmidt.

"Counterattack!" A shout went through the German positions. "Counterattack! Everybody advance!"

"Shit," Voss said with clenched teeth.

"You heard it," said Rauterkus, patting his comrade on the back. Then the sergeant raised his voice: "Counterattack! Everybody follow me!"

"Oh, man," Richards said as he and Voss jumped to their feet.

With their bayonets fixed, the soldiers stormed across the street, past blazing tank wrecks that were emitting toxic smoke, and towards Schmidt, which had belonged to them a day ago. A destructive cocktail of fear and anger now possessed them, which broke out in wild cheers. They had to jump over dead and screaming wounded to get to Schmidt. American medics and even a military chaplain, who administered last rites to the doomed in the midst of the gunpowder steam, cast suspicious glances at the passing Germans.

The counterattack struck the Americans on the wrong foot. Panic broke out on the outskirts of Schmidt when the US infantry accidentally mistook the rolling back Shermans for German tanks. Three officers tried to get the situation under control again when the first salvo of German mortar shells rained down on them with their characteristic whistle. Anyone with enough combat experience knew that they only had one or at most two seconds left to take cover. For an infantryman there was hardly anything worse than mortar fire. For one thing, it was frustrating to be fired at by someone who was too far away for one to return fire. On the other hand, the survival instinct tells one to flee when one is defenseless. There was only one drawback to mortar fire: if one tried to run away, one were most likely hit by smoldering shrapnel, released by every shell that hit the ground, and which shot through the air at an incredible speed. So one had no choice but to grit one's teeth and take cover somewhere. One had to crawl around lying on one's stomach and under no circumstances one was allowed to move upright. All soldiers learned this in their basic training. But especially the freshmen among the Americans forgot this vital lesson in their panic. The shrapnel killed a dozen of them. One of the US officers fired his pistol into the air, but could not stop the soldiers from heedlessly running around. Only in the center of Schmidt the American commanders succeeded in building a new line of defense.

By then the Germans were already moving into Schmidt and occupied a large part of the positions that they had had to abandon the day before. Now several tank wrecks lined the main street, in which fires were crackling.

*

"This is unacceptable, Captain!" Major MacGraw barked angrily. His face was flushed with excitement. "Tell the men to resume the attack at once."

"We must regroup, sir, and then..."

"I gave you an order, Captain!" MacGraw snapped at him. "Immediate counterattack! Do it!"

"Yes, sir."

Again First Lieutenant Miller and his platoon were stricken.

"We'll take the lead," Miller said to his men. "The 3rd Platoon is behind us. Follow me!"

"Move!" Sergeant Clark yelled.

"That's insane," Mellish gasped.

"Well, what will you do?" Copeland returned, rushing forward with the operator and Pellosi, his new ammunition carrier.

37

They worked their way from cover to cover, always ducking and looking for the Germans. Another squad overtook them and started to jump over a pile of rubble when heavy machine gun fire broke out. Three, four, five men collapsed at the same time and rolled down the rubble and onto the road. A GI screamed in panic and staggered back, his face splashed with the blood of his comrades. Hand grenades flew over the rubble and landed in front of the US soldiers.

"Grenade!" Miller yelled in a husky voice and his men threw themselves to the ground. Fortunately they were far enough away.

Three explosions shook the walls of the surrounding ruins.

"God!" Mellish uttered, when he saw what the grenades had done to the comrades of the other squad. They were dead, torn apart as if a pack of rabid hyenas had killed them.

"This is insane, Lieutenant!" Clark gasped, lying in the dirt next to Miller. "The Krauts are shooting us down like rabbits!"

"We got our orders, Sergeant. The major was very clear. He wants this goddamn town and we're gonna get it for him."

"Sure, so he can look good in front of the General!" Clark sneered.

"Stop it, Sergeant!" Miller glared at his subordinate. "Orders are orders, or do we want to talk this out?"

"Yes, sir... I mean... no, sir. But we should at least put blindfolds on these guys, so it would be easier for them."

"Clark, enough!" Miller was obviously upset. The losses did not affect him any less than they did the sergeant. He also thought it was insane for an officer to rush his men into a barrage for the prospect of a commendation from the general and a medal. But after MacGraw gave the order, it became Miller's order. It was not for him to question the order, much less in front of his subordinates. It was that simple in the military.

"Give way, get out of the street! The tanks take the lead," it was heard from behind. A machine gun opened fire on the German position to hold the Krauts down.

"Get those poor guys out of here!" Miller ordered against the noise, pointing at the dead comrades. It was a disgusting task, but no one wanted to be responsible for the dead getting under the tracks of a tank. Miller helped to drag a limp but warm body from the road. He laid it down beside the remains of a wall, staring at his bloodstained hands.

Squeaking and rumbling, five Sherman tanks, lined up like pearls on a string, rolled past him at a decent speed. MacGraw was pressing hard. Machine gun fire rained down on the advancing tanks, but left no lasting impression.

Pellosi shook his head. "I didn't want to be in a steel box like that. They're death traps!"

"Oh, really? And we infantrymen are better off, aren't we?" Copeland asked. He shoved a piece of chewing tobacco in his mouth.

There was a bang, a terrible blow that shook the whole street. A tongue of flame licked up, followed by thick, black smoke.

Pellosi again touched his rosary. "Yes, indeed," he gasped breathlessly.

*

The Germans had not yet been able to re-establish themselves in Schmidt, which had been mostly destroyed, when they heard the tank engines, whose rumble was intensified in the narrow streets. The ground under the soldiers shook, rubble danced around. Dust and mortar broke loose from the masonry and trickled down on them. Fear reached into their hearts, but did not scare even the inexperienced comrades among them as much as before. For most of them, the baptism of fire had been the first step on the way to becoming hardened veterans.

First Lieutenant Drechsler lay in position behind a remnant of a wall. With him were the remaining men of a squad that had once counted 18 men. That was a long time ago. Now only Zöllner, Höffer, Schneider, Grabowski and Mühlstein were left.

NCO Rauterkus rushed over a collapsed building wall together with Richards and Voss and almost jumped on the feet of his company commander.

"Excuse me, Oberleutnant," he gasped.

39

Drechsler waved off. "What about your weapons and ammunition? We have four Panzerfausts and seven hand grenades."

"We have two, and three grenades."

"Let's hope that's enough." Drechsler allowed himself the luxury of a breather lasting several seconds. "Let's go, men! Rauterkus, you take the lead!"

The sergeant nodded and worked his way through the rubble towards the enemy. There was no time for long discussions. So it happened that a sergeant was leading a squad consisting of a first lieutenant and eight soldiers.

The squad reached a good position for an ambush; a wide breakthrough in a house wall, which pointed directly to a sharp bend in the road. Rauterkus threw himself on the dusty floorboards and crawled through the breakthrough into the open. The icy cold reached for him from the underground, touching his heated body which sent shivers down his spine.

"Here come the Tommy boilers."

Drechsler was right behind him. "If we could crack the first one, we'd have a nice roadblock."

"Even better, we let them pass, and then we'll finish off the first and the last," Rauterkus said.

"Good idea. Let's do it your way."

The tracks of the first Sherman crumbled the rubble on the road to dust as the combat vehicle rolled over a pile of ruins. Its cannon lowered almost to the rubble-covered ground as the tank overcame the top of the obstacle. Behind it, the next combat vehicle heaved itself up the mountain of debris. The Chrysler engines roared deafeningly.

Then the first tank stopped abruptly and took fire at a house 30 or 40 yards away. Had the American tank commander recognized a careless movement of a soldier that had been missed by the others?

The already badly damaged house only needed one high-explosive shell from the 75 millimeter cannon to finally collapse and catch fire.

The tank commander, perhaps a little unsatisfied with what he had achieved here, let his Sherman roll on, firing another HE

40

round into the rubble of the house. Rauterkus felt the shock wave of the shot sweep over him and crush him down. For a moment he thought it had blown away all oxygen from the air. He tried to breathe, but his lungs filled with nothing useful. He coughed.

At that moment, a machine gun lodged in the front of the Sherman pumped a long burst of fire into the ruins of another house. Meanwhile, the fifth and last Sherman passed the breakthrough in the wall.

"Watch out," Rauterkus warned as he tucked his Panzerfaust under his right arm and made it ready to fire. He peered through the sight, saw the hull of the tank rolling by in it and pulled the trigger. The warhead hissed away, slammed against the back of the turret while the first Sherman still fired wildly into the surrounding area. The Panzerfaust hit roared through the village, and immediately afterwards a cloud of thick smoke and fire enveloped the Sherman's turret. A bloodcurdling scream drowned out the roar of the engine.

Then the next Panzerfaust warhead rushed towards the most forward tank, drove between the road wheels and hit the thin hull. Immediately flames shot up from the open hatches. Not a single man disembarked; the entire crew was exterminated by the purgatory that was inside the tank.

Hand grenades flew in a high angle against the three remaining combat vehicles, causing lightning but no visible damage.

Suddenly two more hollow-charge projectiles slammed against the steel body of two tanks.

One hit the driver's panel! The Sherman stopped after it had rolled into a dilapidated building. Like a house of cards the walls collapsed above it and buried it underneath. The other warhead sat exactly in the gap between the turret and the hull of the second tank and scored a direct hit. The vehicle began to quake and boil from the inside out. Then it literally bubbled like a saucepan that threatened to overflow, and when ammunition and fuel ignited inside, the turret was torn off in a flash and shot a good five yards into the air before it crashed into the cobblestone pavement.

The last tank fired its main cannon and machine guns wildly without hitting those who had so badly hit its companions. A

41

Panzerfaust hissed like a poisonous snake, but missed the combat vehicle.

First Lieutenant Drechsler reached for the last Panzerfaust, which Mühlstein carried with him. "Give it to me! This is our last one. No matter what this guy does, we're getting out of here!"

The first lieutenant stood behind a projection on the wall, aimed for the broadside of the Sherman and pulled the trigger.

Shot.

Score!

The blast rumbled through the village. The tank jerked, stopped, started smoking, then flames burst out of all openings. Hissing and rattling, the ammunition went up and forced the soldiers to take cover.

"Clean shot, Herr Oberleutnant," Voss said admiringly.

"Thanks." He cleared his throat, a nasty exhaustion tried to paralyze him with all its might. His upper arms ached, the constant shaking from the cold took its toll. "That was good work, men!" he said, using a platitude. "Of all of you."

"Oberleutnant!" One of the soldiers yelled, pointing to a flaming Sherman. Out of the flames three crewmen, blackened with soot, appeared unsteadily. They were burnt, one of the men was literally pulled out of the flames by his comrades. Two more men crawled out of another tank wreck. They staggered away from the steaming combat vehicle as if drunk and threw themselves like children into the next pile of snow.

Rauterkus jumped over the wreckage, his MP40 ready to fire, and confronted the shivering, distraught men. "Hands up! Don't move!"

The Americans had suffered severe burns on their faces and hands, one had been hit by shrapnel. Dazed, some of them raised their hands. One tank driver looked up only briefly as he tried to stop his comrade's bleeding with his burned fingers and a black powdered gauze bandage.

"What are we going to do with them now?" Voss asked after they had taken the prisoners to the protection of that ruin from which they had previously taken the Shermans under fire.

"Shoot them," a harsh voice snarled.

The soldiers flinched and saw Lieutenant Oettinger, who was notably absent during the short fight, and now appeared behind the remains of a wall.

"What?" Richards asked, stunned.

"Shoot them, I say!" Oettinger shook his right fist. "This American scum knows no mercy when they drop bombs on our women and children! They're murderers, all of them!"

One of the younger soldiers nodded in agreement, the others shook their heads, while Drechsler stood there with his mouth open. He didn't think Oettinger had that degree of fanaticism in him.

"Corporal! Shoot these criminals!"

Rauterkus looked at the first lieutenant with grinding jaws, then his eyes fell on the Americans, who looked frightened and exhausted, perhaps not realizing what was going on since they probably do not understand any German.

"I don't think about it!" Rauterkus lowered the muzzle of his submachine gun until it pointed to the floor. "Absolutely out of the question!"

Oettinger turned red with rage. "That was an order, Unteroffizier!"

"But it wasn't my order, Herr Leutnant," Drechsler interrupted. Open disdain dripped from his voice. "Unteroffizier Rauterkus!"

"Here, Herr Oberleutnant."

Drechsler pierced Oettinger with an icy look that was in no way inferior to the coldest nights here in the Hürtgen Forest. "See if the wounded can return to their own lines."

"Jawohl, Herr Oberleutnant!"

Rauterkus went off, while Oettinger could not hide that he considered the intention his company commander had just revealed as scandalous. Then his face turned into a dreadful mask of idolatry. Drechsler knew that he had created a lifelong mortal enemy right in front of him. But he was even more disturbed by his own reaction to this realization: "Fuck it!"

*

43

More and more smoke rose into the sky. They heard the crackling of flames and some secondary explosions and also loud German voices.

"Well, apparently the tanks are done," Copeland commented laconically. "Poor bastards, the guys."

Pellosi kissed his rosary. "I told you, man. These things are nothing but death traps."

All of a sudden, a voice said: "Hey, Americans!"

"What is this?" Mellish wondered.

"Hey, Americans!"

"Ask the Kraut what he wants, Mellish," Clark said to the operator.

"If I have to..." Mellish raised his voice and shouted in German: "What do you want, Kraut?"

"We have five wounded of you," the German replied in pretty good English. "Can we send them over to you?"

Mellish exchanged a surprised look with the Sergeant, who in turn looked at Miller. The Lieutenant shrugged his shoulders, then nodded.

"All right, Kraut!" Clark shouted over. "But no tricks, understand?"

"Understood!" A head with the typical German steel helmet on it appeared on top of the pile of rubble that separated the Krauts from the Americans. The German waved his hand. "We're sending them over now. Help them, they're severely wounded."

Miller waved and Clark and some of his men climbed up the pile of rubble. The German carefully helped a burned tank man climb to the top of the pile of rubble. The Americans picked up the five wounded, helped them move and quickly carried them to the back.

At the top of the pile of rubble, Clark stood face to face with some Germans. If he remembered the enemy insignia correctly, one of the Krauts was a non-commissioned officer. A rather young guy peeked out from under the dirty and bearded face, but his soldiers were all young, too. Blue eyes watched Clark intensively and the sergeant didn't really know how to react to this situation.

"Why?" He asked, following an impulse.

44

The German shrugged his shoulders in a meaningless way. "Why not?"

They looked at each other for a few more seconds, sized each other up silently, then the Kraut just nodded at him. Clark returned the gesture. The German gave him a slight smile, turned around and climbed down the pile of rubble.

Clark turned around, but looked thoughtfully at the German once more before returning to Miller.

"Did the guy say why they let our people go," the first lieutenant asked.

"No, sir." Clark shook his head. "I don't know, but something was strange. I mean, we exchanged wounded with the Germans back in Normandy, but that was through official channels."

"I remember." Miller was thinking. What was that supposed to mean?

*

"Serious charges have been brought against you, Oberleutnant Drechsler," Major Stüttgen began. Drechsler and Rauterkus stood at attention in front of the Major's ammunition box, which had been converted into a desk. "An officer of your company accuses you of high treason."

"Excuse me, Herr Major, but may I know the name of the officer in question?" Drechsler asked very politely.

"The name of the officer is not relevant in this context, Herr Oberleutnant," Stüttgen returned in the same tone of voice.

"I understand, Herr Major."

Rauterkus bit his cheek to keep from grinning. The two officers played by the book, and as the clerk noted on his notepad, no name had been mentioned. But everyone knew that there was only one other officer in the company besides Drechsler.

"I'd like to hear what you have to say about the allegations, Herr Oberleutnant. Is it true you handed prisoners over to the Americans on your own responsibility?"

"That part is true, Herr Major."

45

Stüttgen sucked on the mouthpiece of his pipe. "I would like a more detailed explanation, gentlemen."

"Several factors led to this decision. One was the human factor, since we did not have the resources to provide adequate care for the wounded. However, the military factor alone was decisive in the transfer of the wounded."

"Well?" Stüttgen emitted a small cloud of smoke. "Please elaborate on that."

"The care of such severely wounded men binds a considerable amount of troops and material from the enemy. I decided that leaving the wounded to the enemy would weaken them more than it would help us to keep them in captivity."

"I see." Stüttgen looked at Rauterkus. "Unteroffizier Rauterkus, do you agree with this assessment by your superior officer?"

"Yes, Herr Major."

"I understand," Stüttgen repeated, leaning his back against the basement wall and thinking. He took another puff from his pipe and then nodded. "I can understand your motives very well, gentlemen. And it is frankly impossible for me to see anything like treason in actions that support our war effort and harm that of the enemy. I approve of your actions in hindsight."

Bang!

With this, Stüttgen had averted the accusation of high treason and at the same time had kneed Oettinger in the groin.

"However, I insist that you inform me immediately in a similar situation so that such misunderstandings can be avoided," Stüttgen continued and gave the two men a warning look. "Understood, gentlemen?"

"Yes, Herr Major!" They both replied at the same time.

"Dismissed."

Drechsler and Rauterkus gave a military salute and dismissed. Outside the building, Rauterkus offered the first lieutenant a cigarette.

"Thank you, Karl." Drechsler lit the cigarette before giving his comrade a light. "You were right about Stüttgen."

Rauterkus sucked in the aromatic American tobacco and shrugged his shoulders. "I told you, the major is old school. The old man told us several times about the unofficial Christmas peace of 1914. Nevertheless, it can still backfire. Oettinger's family is of the new high nobility, if you know what I mean. He's not going to take the blame for this."

"Oettinger can go to hell."

Rauterkus raised his eyebrows in surprise. That tone of voice didn't belong to his friend at all.

"I'm fed up with Oettinger and guys like him," Drechsler said quietly. "You can't imagine the nonsense they tell people at home. Sometimes I think we have more in common with the soldiers on the other side than with characters like that."

Rauterkus avoided looking around carefully, but lowered his voice. "That's really close to high treason now, Jupp."

"You think I'm wrong?"

"Not exactly. I just mean you should be careful what you say...even if it sounds weird when I say it." The sergeant grimaced. "I know I have a big mouth, but you've always held back."

"Maybe I was wrong. I'm so sick of this war, Karl. The eternal killing and being killed. It just pisses me off."

"Like all of us."

In silence, they finished smoking and watched the last rays of the sun sink into the Western horizon.

A few Days later

The morning was cold, but not so cold that Sergeant Clark could not do any field exercise with the newly arrived rookies. Of course, utmost caution was advised, because in the dense woods the damned snipers of the Germans were lurking. The US Army had little experience with battles in the mountains or in trenches. The battle-hardened Krauts with their many years of warfare in all imaginable regions had a clear advantage. Clark had to admit this clearly. But the Americans were quick learners – by necessity.

The sergeant walked down the line of his men in the trenches. The veterans seemed to be resigned. Whereas the rookies looked almost paralyzed. They reacted far too slowly when an artillery shell approached. That had to change, so they needed the field exercise.

The sergeant stopped next to a replacement guy who peered across the edge of the trench.

"Keep your head down before a Kraut sees you!"

The boy slid deeper into the trench. "Where are the Germans, Sergeant?"

"Not far away at all! Stay under cover, understand?"

"Yes, Sergeant."

Clark tapped him on the shoulder and kept going. As soon as he disappeared around the next turn of the trench, the boy peered over the edge again.

"Guess you're just dying to show those damn Krauts, huh?" Copeland asked him, shoving the tobacco around in his mouth.

"You betcha."

"Bullshit!" Copeland snapped at the boy, who flinched.

"Bring those Germans over here, let me at 'em...!" the BAR gunman mimicked some fallen comrades. "I've heard it all before!" Copeland hissed. "And what did we hear next? Tell him, Pellosi!"

The Italian-born private had a vicious grin. "How the little boys were crying for their mother while their guts were pouring out of their bellies."

48

"That's right!" Copeland tapped the skinny fellow with his thick finger against his chest. "I'm tired of dragging your dead asses off the battlefield. So do what the Sarge said and keep your head down before it gets shot off!"

Visibly intimidated, the boy crouched down on the bottom of the trench.

"That was a little rough, wasn't it?" Mellish whispered uncertainly.

"He'll survive me hurting his feelings," Copeland grumbled, spitting out a lump of tobacco. "Still better than getting shot in the head. As... as... what was his name? The tall guy with the red hair and the freckles..."

"Nash?" asked Pellosi.

"Was that his name?"

"I think so."

"Was a replacement... like you, too," Copeland said to the boy who was staring at the BAR gunman with eyes as big as saucers. "Always wanted to get the Germans. Couldn't even manage to look at a single Kraut. A sniper blew his brains out first."

The boy looked at the three veterans deeply unsettled, then to the edge of the trench and back to the other GIs.

His neighbor, who had hardly said a word, was fidgeting restlessly.

"What's the matter? Do you have to piss or something?" Copeland asked.

"No, I..." He began hesitantly. "Can I ask you a question?"

The BAR gunman nodded.

"What... what's it like? When you have to fight, I mean?"

Copeland looked down. His face darkened. For days, he and the others that were left lived only in the present. They blocked out all memories, all hopes, desires, fears. At least they tried.

How would it be if you watched your buddy next to you being torn apart by a mine? What was it like when a friend you were talking to just a second ago had his face blown apart in the next second? The bulky Copeland looked into the two frightened faces, but said nothing.

They remained silent for a few minutes, then the second boy started fidgeting again. "I gotta take a piss. Where's the latrine?"

"The latrine is only for shitting," Pellosi informed him. "You can piss in the trench. But keep your head down."

The boy nodded and walked a few yards along the trench. A little embarrassed, he unbuttoned his pants and urinated against the wall.

A wet splash sounded and the boy slipped from the wall of the trench to the ground. The others ducked down immediately as a distant rumble rolled over them. The veterans immediately recognized it as a shot from a large-caliber rifle.

"Holy shit!" Mellish cried out and looked over at the fallen body. No need to worry about his health any more – the back of his head had cracked open like an overripe melon.

"Sheldon?" The other rookie asked, just realizing what had happened. "Oh, my God! Sheldon! Oh, my God! Oh, my God!" He whimpered.

Sergeant Clark stooped around the bend in the trench.

"Shit!" He cursed when he saw what had happened. He waved at Copeland and Pellosi.

"Oh, shit," the BAR gunman growled. He pulled the jacket over the body's head, then grabbed the body by the harness while Pellosi lifted the boots. Together they dragged the corpse to the collection point for the wounded, where the death of the replacement would be officially recorded and neatly entered into the files.

The other rookie had his arms wrapped around him and swayed his upper body back and forth.

"Keep your heads down," Sergeant Clark warned once again in a sharp voice.

*

NCO Rauterkus picked up three very young replacements at the command post and led them to the position of his squad. The experienced soldiers saw them cautiously sneaking through the ruins of Schmidt and started to chatter.

"O Lord, have mercy. Where did they get those boys from? They look as if they should still be at school. Or at home with their mothers sitting at the table." Voss shook his head in disbelief.

"Well, fresh out of basic training," commented Richards. "I bet the boys didn't even have a girlfriend yet."

"I don't think so, too," said Zöllner dryly. "They don't even have to shave yet."

"You didn't have to either when you arrived here, Zöllner," Voss reminded him.

"That was ages ago."

"Just a few weeks."

Zöllner frowned. Was it really just a few weeks ago? It felt much longer. "Anyway, the older one looks like they stole him out of the office. Wanna bet?"

"Nah, dear, I wouldn't bet on it."

Rauterkus guided the three replacements past the wrecks of the American tanks.

"What are those marks?" One of the new men asked, pointing to some chalk markings on the burnt-out Sherman.

"This means that the wrecks have been checked," Rauterkus explained. "And that they are no longer a threat."

"Oh..."

Whatever the boy wanted to say, he fell silent when a gust of wind drove a sweetish smell into his nose. The other new ones also smelled it. They turned pale in an instant.

"My God..." One of them said.

Only now they seemed to understand the full extent of what they saw in front of them – that each of these vehicles had become a fiery grave for its crew.

One boy bent over and threw up.

The veterans saw it.

"Well, this is different from what they tell you at home about the war," Richards commented. "Welcome to ugly reality."

The NCO handed a clean lump of snow to the wheezing boy. He took it in his mouth, chewed it and then spit it out.

"Just like me," remembered Zöllner, shaking his head. Had he really ever been so naive? His head full of stories about the war,

51

of heroic deeds for the Führer, nation and fatherland? Yes. Yes, probably. So much had changed since he had come to the front.

Rauterkus sent the new arrivals into the snowy debris of the house in which the squad had settled.

"Folks, these are Aschenbach, Kleve and Merkel," the NCO introduced. "The three in the front are Voss, Richards and Zöllner."

The three veterans nodded briefly.

Rauterkus pointed to the machine gun nest, which was staffed with four men. Two soldiers peered out of the loophole cut into the wall, one of them with binoculars. The MG42 stood between them on an empty ammunition box, ready to fire. The other two men were playing cards.

"Those are Höffer, Schneider, Grabowski and Mühlstein."

"Mühlstein?" Aschenbach repeated. He was the one who had thrown up. "Isn't that a Jewish name?"

"What a nonsense!" Rauterkus shook his head disapprovingly, anger was visible in the faces of the other veterans. "Name is name!"

"I can reassure you, little one," Mühlstein shouted, grinning broadly. "My family tree can be traced back to the 16th century. We're all Aryan to the foreskin."

The soldiers laughed harshly. Aschenbach turned red.

"What kind of a name is Aschenbach anyway?" Richards asked. "Where are you from, boy?"

"Linz."

"Oh dear," Voss muttered, changing glances with Zöllner, who only shrugged his shoulders.

"Listen," Rauterkus said to the three newcomers. "Stick to the experienced comrades. If they take cover, there is a good reason for that. So you take cover too. Stay close to them. Do what they do."

The NCO looked at Höffer, who was coughing and then spitting a lump of slime into the snow.

"But don't let their bad manners get to you."

The men laughed again.

Something was whistling closer. Alarmed, the veterans looked up.

"Take cover!"

Immediately they threw themselves on their stomachs. Fifty meters away, an American 105 millimeter shell exploded in the treetops. The shock wave gave them a tremendous blow. It was just harassing fire, randomly hitting their positions but causing losses repeatedly.

Rauterkus raised his head to make sure that everyone had taken cover. The only lifted helmet belonged to Richards. The Lance Corporal nodded at him. Rauterkus nodded back. The NCO addressed each man in the group individually to make sure they were all unharmed.

Thus he found the only one who had suffered from the shelling.

Merkel, the oldest of the replacements, stared at the Sergeant with empty eyes. Rauterkus initially believed that the man had only frozen in fear.

"Merkel? Is everything all right?" Rauterkus shook his shoulder. "Hey! Talk to me, man!"

The soldier did not react.

Rauterkus touched his uniform, looking for wounds.

"What is he doing?" Aschenbach asked.

"He's looking for wounds," Zöllner replied.

"I can't find anything," Rauterkus said beside the now trembling Merkel. "Voss! Help me look!"

"Already there!"

Together they turned Merkel to one side and searched the entire body. The face of the soldier lost more and more color and his breath became shallower.

"Where the hell is he hit?" Voss asked angrily, feeling hips and legs. He looked at his fingers, but there was no blood. Merkel's eyes were glassy by now and he seemed to stare into space.

"Where is the wound?" Voss cried furiously.

Rauterkus held Merkel in his arms and took off his Stahlhelm. "Heilige Mutter Maria!"

There was a tiny drop of blood on Merkel's temple, hardly larger than a mosquito bite. The man convulsed, then went limp.

"He's not breathing anymore!"

Merkel uttered a last, tormented sigh, then it was over.

53

Rauterkus pressed his eyes shut.

"What the hell happened to him?" Aschenbach shouted out in horror.

"A shell splinter," Rauterkus replied. "It hit him right under the helmet and then..." The NCO stopped and let Merkel sink gently into the snow.

"But... but... but he can't be dead," Aschenbach stammered.

"But he is dead," Rauterkus sharply replied. "Take away his ammunition and equipment and share it. Then you two carry him to the military hospital in the back."

"The two of us?" Aschenbach asked in shock, pointing to himself and Kleve.

"Yes. You. Both of you." Rauterkus snapped every single syllable between his teeth.

"Yes... yes, Herr Unteroffizier." Intimidated, Aschenbach wanted to salute, but Rauterkus grabbed him by the arm and shoved him to Merkel. They took the dead man's rifle and ammunition and passed it on. Then Aschenbach and Kleve picked up the body with difficulty and staggered backwards with their terrible load.

The veterans looked after them, each one lost in his own thoughts.

The next day

"Here they come again," said First Lieutenant Drechsler to Sergeant Rauterkus standing next to him.

"And I was hoping they had just gone home."

"Unfortunately not."

The American pioneers had cut down the trees at the sides of the narrow forest roads with explosives, creating a broader route for the armored vehicles. Across this, about 20 Shermans and more than 30 half-track vehicles advanced against the German positions in Schmidt. At the sight of the armored armada rolling towards them, the men got scared stiff.

"Where is Leutnant Oettinger?" Voss asked sneeringly.

Richards let out an amused chuckle. "He's sitting in the church tower as usual, sitting on his hands... I mean, he's directing the fire of the mortars," he corrected himself quickly when he felt the sergeant's gaze on him.

"That is also important." Voss grinned at Richards, who poked him in the ribs.

"Shut up," Drechsler ordered.

"Yes, Herr Oberleutnant."

The Shermans fired the first salvo. Explosive rounds ripped the air apart.

"Take cover!"

But the projectiles from the 75 millimeter cannons howled over the crouched soldiers, blowing holes into three already half-destroyed houses in huge eruptions of fire and rocks. A thick wooden beam whirled through the air and slammed almost vertically into the roof of a barn, causing it to collapse. Clouds of dust drifted around, limiting the Germans' view for a few seconds. The Americans used this distraction and moved closer. When they had approached within 400 meters, the order was given to "Fire at will!"

A dozen heavy machine guns and the two 8-8 hidden in the rubble led off.

"Come on, boys! Forward!" Major MacGraw cheered his men as they rushed against Schmidt again. Muzzle flashes flared all over the ruins, and German machine-gunners took his GIs under a murderous barrage.

The men desperately sought shelter behind the tanks, but the MGs kept taking them from the sides. The German gunners reaped a bloody harvest among the Americans. Dozens of soldiers rolled in the snow in pain and cried out for help. A Sherman was hit – probably by a 8-8, MacGraw thought – and disappeared in a cloud of fire, black smoke and metal parts.

The Major hit the sandbags in front of him with his fist. "Call in artillery! The ari should break up the enemy positions!"

"Our men are already very close to the German positions," one of the staff officers remarked. "We're risking hitting our own men, sir."

"We're at war, Captain," MacGraw said curtly. "And in war, you gotta take chances. So let's do it!"

"Yes, sir."

*

An 88 millimeter round hit a Sherman in the rear. The engine compartment blew apart. The next moment, smoke poured out of the open turret hatch. Then a man appeared in a dense cloud of fume, pulled himself up, dropped, rolled down and rolled around on the ground to put out his burning pants. He kicked desperately in the snow. The flames died out and the man crawled dazed behind the smoking tank.

The other combat vehicles fired at the Germans with their coaxial machine guns mounted in the bow. The projectiles bouncing off the debris howled and whistled, they jumped around as ricochets.

The soldiers were lying in the way infantrymen were used to: with their nose in the dirt, their hands clawed in the ground. They made themselves small, didn't dare to raise their heads, waited for their chance. But one of them was unlucky. Zöllner uttered a silent cry and clasped his right forearm, where a ricochet had carved a finger-wide, bloody gash into his flesh. "Scheisse, damn it..." He gritted his teeth and blustered a series of unquotable curses.

Lehmann, the medic, crawled to him while the enemy's constant fire shattered the edges of the cover holes and trenches.

"Is it bad?" Lehmann asked.

"Oh no. It barely scratched the skin."

"Let's have a look. Don't worry, comrade. It'll heal in no time."

The enemy tanks reached the outskirts of Schmidt, smashed down rubble and barricades and entered the village again.

Zöllner could feel the steel colossuses rolling by. The rock-hard frozen ground vibrated. Less than ten steps away, an HE round crashed into the wall of the trench. Splinters hissed howling through the air, some hitting Schneider in the right calf and thigh. Then a shower of earth and stone fragments fell on him. Moaning, he slid down the wall of the trench and looked at his right leg. At first sight the wounds were not life-threatening, but they hurt like hell.

"Schneider's hit," yelled Grabowski. "Medic!"

"Coming!" Lehmann rushed over to tend to the wounded. The ground around him began to tremble, the roaring of another tank engine was approaching at breakneck speed. The medic huddled down to protect Schneider with his own body from the pieces of earth that were loosening from the edge of the trench.

But then he realized that the tank simply wanted to roll over the trench and bury them. Still bullets whipped over them.

"Lehmann! Schneider! Get away!"

If Lehmann jumped up, he'd be perforated before he even took three steps. But the medic couldn't abandon his wounded comrade. There was no time left. The outline of the Sherman appeared on the edge of the trench...

*

Not 20 steps to the right of it Rauterkus and Voss squatted behind the wreckage of a combat vehicle destroyed days ago. Right in front of them, the Sherman was heading for the hole of Schneider, rotating above him and Lehmann, as if to crush his comrades alive like a raging beast.

Voss and Rauterkus each had one of the few remaining Panzerfausts.

"Aim low at the tracks," Rauterkus instructed.

"Understood."

"Ready... go!"

The two men jumped out from behind the wreckage and fired the hollow charge warheads. Explosions flared up on the right side of the Sherman, the tread broke. The monster stopped.

At that moment the bow machine gun of a tank driving in second row started to spit fire. At first the impacts were directly on the first Sherman, buzzed away as ricochets and then chased over to the tank wreck that Voss and Rauterkus had served as cover until then.

The NCO threw himself forward, diving behind the wrecked Sherman. Voss was less lucky. A bullet pierced his left thigh and the lance corporal fell headfirst into the snow. Immediately he screamed in pain as Rauterkus' hand grabbed his harness and dragged him into cover.

First Lieutenant Drechsler saw just that much before a tongue of flame hissed from the turret hatch of the next Sherman. With a terrible roar, reminiscent of a rumbling volcano, a pillar of blaze shot up and tore the turret off the tank. The heat of the explosion swept over Drechsler. The 8-8 had scored the next direct hit.

The lieutenant knocked the snow from his uniform, shook like a dog and rubbed his ears, which were ringing. Thereupon he tried to get an overview of the battle that was raging in his front section.

He caught his breath.

Wave after wave and despite their losses, the Americans ran against his lines.

Unstoppable.

There were just too many.

"Back to the second line! Back to the second line!"

*

"Go, go, go!" Sergeant Clark shouted as the men in his squad moved into the positions just abandoned by the Germans.

Mellish landed beside him in the trench and stepped on something soft. He looked down and stared at bloody flesh. A German had been shredded to pieces in his foxhole.

God, why is this happening to me, he thought to himself.

Machine guns were rattling, covering every free space between the rubble and tearing holes in the ground. Ice and stones were hurled up between five GIs. Two men fell and stopped moving. A German mortar round penetrated the frozen ground behind Mellish and the sergeant and blew up. Dirt rained down on them.

Then screams were heard: "Medic! Medic! Over here, goddamn it!"

Clark lifted his head up carefully and looked out into the desert of debris that was once a small German town. From a hole in the house wall opposite, the typical muzzle flash of a German MG42 flickered up. 7.92 millimeter rounds swept across the captured trench, shredding the sandbags at the edges and forcing the sergeant into cover.

"Grenades! We'll ice that goddamn machine gunner!"

"Whatever you say, Sarge."

He and Mellish pulled out grenades, pulled the pin and threw them high into the machine gun positions. One landed on target, and a German shout was heard. Then the grenade exploded and the machine gun stopped barking.

Behind them a Sherman received a hit from an 8-8. The tank disappeared in a cloud of fume. As it disappeared, the two men stared at the turretless steel torso from which flames belched up meter-high into the sky.

"Mellish!" The voice of First Lieutenant Miller was heard through the roar.

"Here, sir!"

"Report to the tanks! Tell them to pull back! Those things aren't worth a damn here!"

"I'll pass it right through, Lieutenant."

59

The operator made the report. The tank driver on the other end of the line was clearly relieved that he was allowed to leave this witch's cauldron. More than half of the Sherman tanks involved were now on the battlefield as burning heaps of scrap metal. The tanks gathered outside Schmidt and supported the infantry as best they could with fire from their cannons and machine guns. However, because of all the debris they could hardly do anything.

"We advance!" Miller shouted. "Everybody advance!"

"Everybody advance!" Sergeant Clark repeated. "Come on, Mellish!"

"Coming, Sarge!"

The operator climbed out of the trench and followed his squad. He rushed over the debris in zigzags. Another machine gun rattled off, bullets whizzing around him.

"Ah, shit! Shit! Shit!" The operator cursed and changed direction quickly. As a result, he ran into a different alley than his fellow soldiers, but the tracer bullets missed him. With muffled sounds they drilled into the walls of the surrounding ruins. Before the shooters could realign their weapon, Mellish reached the ruins of an apartment building and was safe. The operator would have liked to break out in loud cheers of relief.

"I'm alive. I'm alive," he whispered to himself.

He took several deep breaths and looked around. None of his squad was to be seen. He was alone.

"Not good," said Mellish, who was prone to talk to himself. "Not good at all."

Something was whistling towards him. The operator had been so distracted that he heard the damn grenade too late. An explosion flashed up behind him and he felt something sharp enter his body. Immediately Mellish was smashed against the wall by the shock wave. It became dark around him.

*

At the top of the church tower, Lieutenant Oettinger watched as the Americans took the first line of defense despite all the losses. The German troops withdrew to the second line. Oettinger put down his binoculars and turned to the corporal who was sitting by the field telephones.

"Report to the mortars: Put barrage fire on the Western entrance to the town! Quickly!"

"Jawohl, Herr Leutnant. Put barrage fire on the Western entrance to the town," the corporal repeated, already holding the receiver to his ear.

Oettinger grunted and looked through the binoculars again. Since Major Stüttgen had dismissed the accusation of high treason against Drechsler and Rauterkus, the lieutenant moved only on tiptoes. He did not want to arouse further displeasure. At least not yet. He would wait for his chance. And it would come. Those arrogant guys, so convinced of themselves, would find out that it could go the other way! Someone would listen to him and take what he had to say seriously. It is quite possible that Stüttgen would then also been thrown to the wolves. But perhaps the Americans would also do Oettinger a service and settle the whole matter in his favor.

The lieutenant dismissed this jet-black mind game with an inward shrug of his shoulders and continued to observe the entrance to Schmidt through binoculars. On the outskirts of the town a good dozen enemy combat vehicles gathered. From there they could not do much against the comrades who had hidden in the debris.

Stupid Americans.

Oettinger saw the turret of three Shermans spinning. He frowned.

What are they aiming at?

An icy terror ran through him as the gun barrels rose steeply upwards and aimed right at the steeple.

Right at him.

Apparently one of the tank commanders had spotted either him or the light reflexes from his binoculars and decided to eliminate the enemy observer. This discovery paralyzed Oettinger for the time of a heartbeat.

"Don't..." He said, and then it was all over.

61

The thundering from the tank guns shook the village. The steeple exploded in a huge eruption of fire and dust. The top sagged to the side and crashed into the street with a blast. For seconds all of Schmidt was enveloped in a huge cloud of dirt and debris.

*

"Mellish!" First Lieutenant Miller yelled as more and more artillery shells rained down on Schmidt. "That's our own goddamn ari pounding us into the ground here! They should just cease fire! Mellish? Where the fuck is Mellish?"

"I don't know, sir. He was just beside me a moment ago," Sergeant Clark yelled in the roar of the full-automatic fire.

A shock wave swept through the alleyway, pressing the men to the ground.

"Holy shit!" Copeland shouted out. "What the fuck was that?"

"Somebody smashed the steeple!" Burns called back and wiped the dirt out of his eyes. "Hey, over there!"

The medic pointed to an alleyway.

"What's there?" Clark asked.

"There's Mellish! Shit, two Krauts are with him! They're taking him away!"

Indeed! Two field gray figures grabbed the radio operator and dragged his motionless body with them.

"Motherfucker!" Copeland fired his BAR at the Germans. The bullets missed their target, entered harmlessly into a wall of a building.

"Are you crazy, Copeland? Cease fire!" Clark screamed at him angrily.

"Do you want to hit Mellish, you idiot?" Pellosi yelled at him too.

"Those goddamn Krauts are gonna kill him, Sarge," Copeland shrieked. "Mellish is a Jew, goddamn it! We know what those sons of bitches will do to him!"

"They won't!" Miller put a new magazine in his Thompson. "Because we're gonna get him out of there! Follow me!"

The lieutenant jumped up and the squad followed him. They ran to the spot where the Germans had disappeared with Mellish behind a half collapsed wall. Carefully they worked their way forward and entered a house. Dropped down plaster crunched under their boots. They climbed over a heap of piled up ceiling beams.

"There's nothing here, Sarge!" Copeland shouted.

"Blood," Burns said, pointing to a fresh trail of red speckles.

"Pellosi, you lead the way."

"Understood, Sarge."

Pellosi continued to advance with his Garand at the ready. "That's the way down to the basement," he finally reported.

"Watch out!" Sergeant Clark suspiciously watched the dark basement entrance. "Careful now!"

They lined up around the basement entrance when a heavy artillery shell exploded close to the ruins of the house. The tremor rocked the remains of the building, making it creak. Then the ground beneath them gave way and they fell down.

*

All around, the clattering of handguns and machine guns could be heard, grenades howled through the air and exploded with a cracking sound.

Sergeant Rauterkus put Voss, who was still screaming in pain, down and waved Grabowski and Aschenbach towards him.

"Take him to the assembly point in the cellar over there!"

"Yes, Unteroffizier."

The two soldiers picked up the wounded comrade and brought him to safety.

"Rauterkus!" Drechsler shouted over the racket. "Were those the last of them? Ari is smashing everything to bits. We must go to the cellar!"

The sergeant looked around and discovered Lehmann kneeling over a collapsed figure.

"There's Lehmann! I'll get him! Go down!"

Rauterkus hurried over to the medic.

"Lehmann! Get out of the street! Ari is going to smash everything!"

As if to underline the sergeant's words, a tremendous shock swept through the alley and knocked them off their feet.

"I can't leave him lying here," the medic shouted as he picked himself up and took care of the wounded man again.

"You stubborn asshole!" Rauterkus shouted at him and only now he saw that the wounded man was an American. "This can't be happening!"

He pulled out his knife and cut the straps of the haversack radio, whose shattered remains were hanging on the American's back.

"Grab him and get out of here!"

They grabbed the wounded man by the arms and dragged him with them. A machine gun quacked, bullets flew around them, tore the plaster out of the wall next to them. Somebody bellowed.

They reached the dilapidated house, climbed over the rubble and then down the stairs to the basement.

"Who do you have there?" Höffer asked.

"Someone who got hit badly," Lehmann replied curtly.

"That's a Yank!"

"Well?"

"I'm just saying..."

Höffer looked at Rauterkus, who only shook his head briefly. "Don't ask."

A tremendous detonation shook the whole basement and when the ceiling crunched, everyone looked up in concern.

Then, with a loud crash, part of the ceiling came down. Dust enveloped everyone, making the men cough and choke.

Only slowly something could be seen in the faint glow of the storm lanterns. Several dusty grey figures lay on the rubble, trying to free themselves from the tangle of limbs.

Mühlstein had to laugh despite everything: "They got it all mixed up."

Rauterkus hurried over and pulled the upper man by the arm.

"Is everything all right with... "

The sergeant fell silent when he realized that the man he was holding by the arm was an American soldier.

At that same moment, the American also realized who he was dealing with.

64

In a reflex action, they both grabbed their hip and ripped the gun from its holster. In the next second, both had the barrel of a .45 Colt in front of their noses.

"Americans!"

"Germans!"

Everyone was shouting.

Weapons were raised, index fingers wrapped around the triggers.

The soldiers were in a stalemate. Seconds passed that seemed like an eternity. No one spoke a word or dared to move a muscle. It was clear to everyone that a firefight in this narrow basement would lead to a bloody massacre.

The sergeant at Rauterkus' feet blinked in confusion as he saw the muzzle of the American Colt in front of his face. Then his gaze sought that of the sergeant and he opened his eyes in surprise.

"You? You again?"

"The sergeant?"

"Karl?" Drechsler demanded an explanation.

"This is the sergeant to whom we delivered the wounded tank drivers," Rauterkus informed. To shoot this man now... no, that would be wrong. It just felt wrong.

Very slowly, Rauterkus pulled back his pistol and lowered the muzzle towards the ground. It was an impulsive decision from the gut that he had not thought through.

The US sergeant looked at him. Surprise was in his eyes. For a few seconds he struggled with himself, but then he also lowered his gun.

"Karl?"

"Everything's all right."

"Clark?"

"I'm fine, sir."

Another tremor made everyone flinch, almost causing them to open fire on each other. More dust and mortar dripped down from the ceiling, the soldiers of both nationalities coughed.

"Somebody help me here or we'll lose the boy," Lehmann said. His hands were bloody up to his elbows. The medic had been caring for the wounded American the whole time.

Burns raised his head. "Sir, they're taking care of Mellish. Request permission to assist the German medic."

"Burns, you..." Miller started hot-tempered and looked over to the Germans. Their officer was eyeing him very fiercely. Then he let his MP40 slide sideways on his belt until the barrel pointed down. The Kraut nodded at him.

"Damn it, Burns! Okay, go." Miller also pointed his Thompson at the ground.

"Sir?" Copeland asked uncertainly. The burly machine gunner had still not been able to pull his BAR out from under the rubble and was only holding the gun in his hand.

"Sir!"

"What, Copeland?"

"What... What are we doing here, sir?"

If only Miller knew.

More impacts caused the floor to shake. More and more guns of all calibers fired at Schmidt. Shaken like in an earthquake, the vaults of the half-collapsed basement rocked. Continuously, explosions thundered through the village in the Hürtgen Forest.

The two medics no longer paid attention to their surroundings, concentrating solely on their task. They understood each other without many words. Burns pulled a small sachet from his medical bag.

"Sulfonamide."

"Ah."

The two of them spread the powder on the radio operator's torn back. The heavy haversack had caught some of the shrapnel, barely saving Mellish's life.

Finally, the medics applied a bandage. The operator groaned and moaned, his eyes half-opened and he began to whimper in pain.

Lehmann pulled out a syringe.

"Morphine."

"Okay."

Lehmann injected a shot and Mellish passed out again.

"How do we know this guy won't kill Mellish?" Copeland hissed.

"Because I'm a medic," Lehmann replied in English, without taking his eyes off Mellish. "I'm not killing anybody!"

"Sure you do! All Krauts are murderers! Always have been! Every kid knows that," Copeland snapped back harshly. The gunner from Mississippi did not know anything about awkwardness, but he was surprised that the German had understood him.

"And all Yanks are either criminals from New York or primitive rednecks from the South, right?" Rauterkus asked in English.

Copeland looked at him wide-eyed, his lower jaw dropping with amazement. For the first time he was speechless.

"The Kraut's got you good, eh, Copeland?" Pellosi snorted. The tension was beginning to ease.

"Shut up, Pellosi!"

Some of the boys laughed softly, others had to wait for the translation, then grinned weakly. But this did not prevent them from nervously stroking their gun and never keeping their fingers too far away from the trigger. The only exception were the two medics who treated Mellish's wounds hand in hand. In doing so, they were as skilled as if they had always worked closely together.

The other men watched with mixed feelings as the medics treated Mellish.

"Fine," Burns said. "I think we've done everything we can do so far."

"Ja," Lehmann agreed, "but still the man should be moved to a hospital as soon as possible. I'm worried about internal bleeding."

"You're right about that."

In a corner of the basement, Voss gave a moan. His face was pale with pain, thick beads of sweat were on his forehead and upper lip. The emergency bandage on his thigh was soaked in blood.

"Lehmann, Voss is not doing particularly well," Höffer said who was worried about his friend.

"Can you manage it alone?" Burns asked.

"Yes, go."

The American medic hurried to Voss, accompanied by partly disbelieving looks from the present Germans and GIs.

Meanwhile, First Lieutenant Drechsler watched his American counterpart. He had the face of a movie actor and looked back at him. Very slowly, so as not to cause any misunderstandings, Drechsler pulled the cigarette pack out of his uniform and put a cigarette butt between his lips. Following an impulse he offered one to his counterpart.

The American officer with the face of an actor hesitated for a moment but then took a cigarette. Drechsler gave him a light and finally lit his own cigarette.

"Herr... Herr Oberleutnant..." Aschenbach's timid voice was heard.

"Yes?"

"What... I mean, what do we do now?"

"We're smoking a cigarette, Private."

Aschenbach was at least a bit confused. But the other men in the cellar felt the same. No one had prepared them for such a situation.

Young Aschenbach took heart and tried again: "Are we prisoners, Herr Oberleutnant?"

"No, we are not."

The Americans, who understood German, raised their heads reflexively. Fingers felt their way back towards the trigger of various weapons.

"Then... are the Americans our prisoners?"

"No, the Americans are not our prisoners either," Drechsler said loud and clear.

Those fingers near a trigger relaxed again, which the Lieutenant did not fail to notice.

"So what now?"

"We wait."

"In Africa we once had to wait a whole night," Rauterkus said. "We were on patrol and met some Tommies in this oasis when the shelling started from both sides."

"Yes, it was a bit crazy," Drechsler remembered. "We were all sitting in the holes together, waiting for the chance to move on."

Astonished looks were exchanged.

"Um," Mühlstein began, "and then what happened, Herr Oberleutnant?"

"In the morning, we shook hands and returned to our lines."

"Just like that?"

"Just like that," Drechsler confirmed.

Copeland slid back and forth trying to find a more comfortable seating position, shaking his head. "Crazy Germans," he muttered.

"Not as crazy as an opossum hunter from the South," Lehmann said.

"Huh?" Copeland stared at the Kraut with his mouth open.

"You're from the South. I can hear it in the way you talk."

"And how do you know that, Kraut?"

"Spent almost a year with relatives in America before the war. Very nice people."

Copeland pulled out his tobacco box and stuck some chewing tobacco in his mouth.

"Hmph," the machine gunner said. "Where have you been?"

"Redding, Philadelphia."

That part of town was almost exclusively populated by German immigrants.

The GIs were quite impressed that one of their enemies had visited their country. It was obvious.

"Then why are you fighting for Hitler?" Pellosi wanted to know.

"We are fighting for our country," Rauterkus clarified. "For our families. For our brothers."

He pointed to his comrades.

The GIs exchanged thoughtful looks. Each of them could understand this.

"It's a crazy war," Clark finally said.

Rauterkus had a dry laugh: "Yes."

"Your wounded man is doing well so far," Burns reported, who had treated Voss' wound. "But he, too, is in dire need of a military hospital."

"A lot more boys will have to go there," Lehmann said, pointing to the ceiling. "The shelling is subsiding. There will be many wounded."

"Well," Burns said slowly. "We've got some room here..."

Lehmann tilted his head to one side. "He has a point, Herr Oberleutnant."

The officers looked at each other.

"And what do we do now?"

69

*

It wasn't planned. It was improvised. It was just plain crazy.

"That's just insane," Copeland ranted angrily. "We could be up against the wall for this!"

"They're gonna put us up against the wall for this," Höffer feared too.

The two very different men looked each other in the eyes.

"But we can't just leave the poor guys lying there," Höffer added.

"No, we can't."

When the barrage subsided, Schmidt looked like a heap of debris. Hardly one stone had remained on top of another.

Wounded men of both sides lay everywhere: men with injuries to their heads, arms or legs, with torn limbs and bloody bodies. Many were screaming and writhing in pain, others lay very still, their faces pale as wax. Experienced soldiers knew that especially the silent ones had hardly any chance to survive the next night. Cries of pain and prayers were heard from time to time.

Copeland spat his chewing tobacco in the snow and rubbed his fingers that were frozen in the cold. "Fucking shit."

Somebody nearby was whimpering. "Help. Help me," a thin voice begged.

A young German grenadier, maybe eighteen years old, lay just around the corner.

"I've been hit," the boy gritted his teeth. "My stomach..."

A splinter had opened his abdominal wall like a scalpel. With both hands firmly pressed against the ghastly wound, he tried to keep his intestines inside. Only now the boy realized that an American was crouching before him.

"No, please... please don't shoot me," the grenadier begged. "Please don't..."

They are as afraid of us as we are of them, Copeland thought.

"I won't hurt you," he tried to calm the grenadier and tore open his first aid kit. "Let me help you. Hey, come over here."

Höffer hurried over and swore softly. "Scheisse."

"Can we do anything?"

"I'll give him morphine," Höffer said and gave the boy a shot.

70

With his fading senses, the grenadier was still trying to grasp a situation in which a German and an American soldier had come to his aid. He was shaken by a convulsion, bloody foam was coming out of his mouth and nose.

"Mum," he exclaimed. "Mum, I want to go home..."

Together, Höffer and Copeland tried to stop the bleeding, though it seemed to be in vain. All they could do was hope for a miracle. But a miracle did not happen. The boy's eyes blurred like the air on a cold evening. Despite the anesthetic, he managed to claw his bloody fingers to Copeland's sleeve. His clouded eyes were looking upwards, as if he could see something up there.

"Mum... Mum..."

The two men felt life slipping away from the battered body. All that remained was a bloody shell.

For quite a while Höffer and Copeland continued to squat beside the body. It struck even the hardest cynic to the core when a dying man became a little boy again, crying for his mother. No, such an experience left no one unmoved.

Copeland had never been a great thinker and he knew it. But now he was forced to ask questions. They had been trained to see the Germans as bloodthirsty Huns, rabid dogs, monsters to be shot down. Apparently, the opposite was also the case. But the death of the young German soldier now prompted him to ask himself:

What are we doing here?

Why are we killing each other?

"We..." Höffer broke off and swallowed the lump in his throat. "We have to move on. Help where we can."

"Yes." Copeland took a deep breath. "Yes, we gotta."

*

"You are completely insane, man."

It was the first time Sergeant Rauterkus heard Major Stüttgen raise his voice. And then, right away, so impressive.

71

"I beg your pardon, Herr Major, but Herr Major wanted to be informed if something ... extraordinary would happen again," First Lieutenant Drechsler replied submissively.

"Extraordinary? Are you kidding me, Herr Oberleutnant?" Stüttgen shouted with reddened cheeks.

"Of course not, Herr Major," Drechsler hurried to assure.

Stüttgen gave an angry snort. After Schmidt had been largely leveled to the ground by the severe battles, the Major had moved his command post to the Mestrenger Mill. From here he could see a large part of the battlefield and of course he knew how fiercely the fight for Schmidt had been.

Stüttgen stared at the rough wood of the empty ammunition box, which once again served as his desk. He rubbed his thumb across the uneven surface, but he was unable to get any inspiration to help him out of this mess.

"What you are doing is fraternizing with the enemy," Stüttgen finally said soberly. "Anyway, some office sitter in the back room could tell us that!"

Rauterkus almost gave a sigh of relief. The major had spoken of "us", so they could hope that he stood by them.

Stüttgen pulled out his pipe with mechanical movements and began to stuff tobacco into it.

"Report again from the beginning," he asked curtly.

"Jawohl, Herr Major. After the shelling ceased, we began to care for our wounded. Of course, we also took care of the wounded of the enemy. It turned out that our medics were caring for Americans and American medics for our men. And then there was the suggestion that a temporary assembly point for the wounded could be set up. Since there were hardly any buildings left intact, Americans and Germans were brought together ... for strictly practical reasons, of course," Drechsler explained.

"Of course."

Amazing, Rauterkus thought to himself, how much sarcasm the Major can put into those two words. But since Jupp did not take the truth too seriously, that is quite understandable...

"Due to the large number of wounded, it became clear that more help was needed," Drechsler continued. "We tried to get it."

"How many wounded are in Schmidt?" Stüttgen asked, lighting his pipe.

"I can't give you exact numbers, Herr Major, but Doctor Rösler estimates that..."

"Doctor Rösler?" Stüttgen interrupted the lieutenant with a deep furrow in his forehead. "Our Doctor Rösler? The regimental doctor?"

"Jawohl, Herr Major."

Stüttgen blew out a cloud of smoke. "When did you call in the regimental doctor?"

"As I mentioned before, more help was needed for the wounded. And the regimental doctor seemed the most suitable person for the job."

"And after you had organized all this, including the cooperation with the Americans, you thought it was time to tell your commander about the whole matter, right?" Stüttgen asked snappily.

"Well, not quite, Herr Major."

Stüttgen snorted again and sucked on his pipe. He sucked in the smoke and then let it slowly out again. "You were about to report how many wounded are lying in Schmidt."

"According to Doctor Rösler's estimate, just over 500."

The commander nearly choked on his pipe shaft.

"500?" He repeated in disbelief.

"Yes, Herr Major. However, more wounded are constantly being brought to the assembly point, so there will be many more by now. And that in the freezing cold."

"Do we have any bandages left?"

"We're almost out. But the Americans are better off. So if we split up the material... "

"I see." The Major straightened his upper body, then he grinned. "Well, since it appears that everyone else is involved in this operation except me, let's get this right. And by that I mean that we don't all end up in summary court martial."

"Yes, Herr Major," Drechsler and Rauterkus replied at the same time.

"One more thing." The major rummaged around in his rucksack and pulled out a bottle of French cognac and three small glasses.

He unscrewed the bottle and poured each of them to the width of two fingers. Heaven alone knew where he got that bottle. The times were long ago when French loot was traded.

"I've been saving this one for a special occasion. So let's drink, gentlemen, while we still can."

Stüttgen handed Drechsler and Rauterkus a glass. "To a prompt ending of the war. And to not being put up against the wall. Cheers!"

May 1945

"The war is over! The war is over!"

Shouting loudly, Aschenbach raced from behind towards the poor defensive line of soldiers, who had taken up position behind the low wall of a farmhouse.

Hollow-cheeked, bearded faces turned to the lance corporal, who waved a note back and forth.

"What are you talking about?" Mühlstein wanted to know.

"The war is over!" The young soldier was almost going crazy with excitement, or so it sounded. "Dönitz has announced unconditional surrender!"

The other men said nothing. They didn't even move, they just stared. Maybe they didn't even understand what they heard.

"Where did you get this, Aschenbach?" Captain Drechsler asked. After all, they had had no contact with other units for two days.

"A messenger came by bicycle. Since the night of May 8th to 9th there has been an official cease-fire! Here is the message, Herr Hauptmann. It's over."

"It's over," Drechsler repeated tonelessly. Then he read what the piece of paper said. There it was, in black and white.

"It's over."

The message spread through the group of men. Only 17 were left.

The forever non-commissioned officer Rauterkus took off his helmet and ran his hand through his hair. "Over and done with."

"And all that shit for nothing," Richards moaned.

"What are we gonna do now?" Grabowski shook his head. "I mean, that's the next question, right?"

"First, we wait," Drechsler said. "And wait for what is coming. No sense taking any unnecessary risks now."

The men remained brooding silently over their situation and their uncertain fate. Then the first ones began to make plans.

"I think I will become a mason," Aschenbach announced. "There's so much to rebuild, we'll need many masons, right?"

"That's right," Grabowski confirmed. "I was an electrician before the war. They will be needed too."

"A car is coming!" Mühlstein, who had kept an eye on the dirt road, shouted. "The guy in the back seat is holding up a white flag!"

"Stay calm, men," Drechsler warned. "Nobody is going to shoot until I give the order! Understand?"

"Understood, Hauptmann."

The vehicle, an American Willy-type SUV, was bouncing up the dirt road. Next to the driver and the GI in the back seat, there was a first lieutenant in the vehicle.

"They're very self-confident," Kleve muttered.

Rauterkus shrugged. "They sure can."

The car stopped 15 meters in front of the farmhouse and the American officer got out.

"Who is in command?" He asked in German.

"That would be me. Hauptmann Drechsler."

The American officer greeted him. "First Lieutenant Brown, sir. As you probably already know, the war is over."

"Yes, we heard," Drechsler confirmed soberly.

"I must urge you to submit to my captivity, Captain."

So it was official.

Captain Drechsler looked at the poor little lot who were calling themselves "battalion" on the paper. "Unteroffizier Rauterkus, let the men report for duty."

"Yes, Herr Hauptmann," Rauterkus confirmed, greeting with a hand on his forehead.

Drechsler returned the greeting and watched as the sergeant ordered the men to line up in two rows. Then he returned and greeted the captain again. "Herr Hauptmann, the men have reported for duty."

"Thank you, Unteroffizier."

Drechsler put his hand on the edge of the cap. "Men, we are now going into captivity. We fought together, now we will also walk together the hardest way of a soldier. I thank you for all that you have done."

With these three short sentences, Drechsler had said more than a whole book could have said. It was a throat-clenching experience for the soldiers.

The captain turned to the American officer. The first lieutenant had watched everything with interest and snapped to attention.

"First Lieutenant Brown, Captain Drechsler and his battalion will enter into your captivity."

The two officers saluted each other. Brown then looked past the captain to the few soldiers.

"Uh, Captain, where's the rest of your battalion?"

"The rest?" Drechsler felt a big lump in his throat. "That's all that's left."

In disbelief, Brown stared at the few filthy men in front of him. He opened his mouth, but said nothing.

He saluted again and Drechsler returned the salute.

An US Army truck rolled down the dirt road. The men were about to be taken to a prison camp.

The post-war Period

The end of the war was not an improvement for everyone. In the infamous Rheinwiesen camps, the prisoners of war died of hunger, hopelessness and arbitrariness of the guards. Camp life on bare earth and the lack of sanitary facilities contributed to the spread of diseases. Hardly a morning went by without dozens of prisoners being found dead in the mud. In the first three months, hundreds and thousands were struck by this fate.

Grabowski got pneumonia and died a short time later because no medicine was available.

Höffer drowned when his burrow collapsed after days of rain and buried him.

Aschenbach tried to get hold of a piece of bread lying in the dirt near the fence and caught the bullet of a guard post.

Mühlstein refused to give away his wedding ring, whereupon the US soldier, who already wore four watches and three rings on his hands and wrists, shot away his lower jaw. Mühlstein died two days later.

Only very gradually the camp guards changed their behavior, and the prisoners were either released or transferred to other camps.

Many soldiers shed bitter tears when films from the concentration camps were shown to them as part of their political re-education. Only the ones who were completely blinded by ideology still refused to accept the truth. These were the ones who had to remain in the camps. The prisoners who were classified as harmless were released after a few months. Among them were Drechsler and Rauterkus.

The time that followed was very difficult for all of them. The whole of Germany laid in ruins. Hunger and hopelessness were constant companions of the population.

Germany was divided into four occupation zones. And soon a new conflict arose: East against West.

Finding work proved to be difficult for former soldiers. In many places companies refused to hire the men. A construction company in a small Westphalian town was no exception.

"You are militarists," Dieter Uhl, the company's managing director, explained to them with a malicious smile on his lips. "And we don't want people like that in here."

"Strange," Rauterkus said, whose eyes sparkled dangerously. "You've built bunkers, bridges and I don't know what else for the Wehrmacht and made a lot of money from it. And now you won't even hire us?"

Uhl went dark. "How dare you?"

"By the way," Rauterkus continued unmoved, "what happened to your brown uniform and the fancy party badge, Uhl?"

The head of the secretary in the front part of the office turned around.

The manager, however, flinched back, turned chalk-white, and looked flabbergasted.

"Who are you?" Uhl whispered startled.

"Think hard, Uhl. Who was it that broke your jaw?"

Uhl hadn't recognized his old opponents in these two rugged looking men. However, it was very interesting to see how quickly Uhl's face could change from an unhealthy cheese white to a hearty flush of anger. Anyway, the job interview was over and a little later the two friends were standing in front of the door, followed by harsh swearwords and curses.

"They won't hire us here anymore," Drechsler noted. "Insulting the boss was a great help in our job interview. Well done, Karl."

"At least I didn't punch him in the teeth," Rauterkus pondered with a broad grin. "This time it was you, Jupp."

"Sorry, but it was long overdue. That stupid dung beetle! He keeps falling on his feet!"

"Well," Rauterkus said, "vermin is hard to get rid of."

"That's true, but what are we going to do now?"

"Something will work out."

Actually, something did work out. A few days later they met Voss and went to the village inn run by Drechsler's family. It hadn't been affected by the war.

79

Behind the bar were Drechsler's father and sister.

"Here, for you, guys. First round is on the house."

"Thanks, dad." The younger Drechsler looked at his friend. "When are you going to propose to Sabine, Karl? You've been putting it off for years."

"First a damn world war came along, and now we have no work. So there's no chance of getting married."

"Sabine doesn't think so."

"Change the subject, please."

Voss giggled into his beer glass. "You really act like brothers."

"After all we've been through together, we are brothers," Rauterkus said.

"That's true." Voss drank a big sip of beer. "So let's get back to the job. I heard that they are looking for people with military experience again."

"But not the French Foreign Legion again!" Drechsler was disgusted. "All the Nazis went there. I want nothing to do with them anymore!"

"Neither do I, Joseph. Calm down," Voss said. "No, it's something new. It's called the Federal Border Guard."

"And what should the Federal Border Guard do?"

"Well, protect the borders, I would say," Voss said and laughed when he saw the pinched faces of his friends. "We can't all study medicine like Lehmann, can we?"

"No, we can't," Drechsler sighed.

"So let's have a look at the Federal Border Guard?"

"Sure. It's better than working part-time as a construction worker."

*

The Korean War, which broke out five years after the end of the Second World War, led to a further intensification of what was now called the "Cold War". And the Western Allies realized that they needed the still young German Federal Republic in their ranks if there ever was to be an open conflict between East and West.

80

So finally new German armed forces were formed: the Bundeswehr.

Spring 1957

"The recruits have reported, Herr Hauptmann," Sergeant Voss announced to his company commander and stood according to the regulations.

"Thank you, Herr Oberfeldwebel," Captain Rauterkus replied and returned the greeting with practiced nonchalance. Then he turned to the recruits.

"Good morning, men!"

"Good morning, Herr Hauptmann," they replied cautiously.

"Well, some are still asleep," Rauterkus grinned. "We can do better than that, can't we? Good morning, men!"

"Good morning, Herr Hauptmann!" It echoed back.

"Very well, that sounds much better," Rauterkus said in a good mood. "At ease, men!"

The company followed the order.

"Today is a special day for us, comrades. The battalion commander, Oberst Drechsler, is visiting with some American officers to get an idea of the state of the troop. So today we will march to the firing range and give the high ranking visitors a small sample of our skills at the gun. However, I would like to ask for extreme caution. An accident is the last thing we need, comrades, so care is the order of the day."

Out of the corner of his eye, the captain spotted three approaching vehicles and turned his head. In the open jeep, driving at the head of a column of vehicles, he saw the battalion commander.

"ATTENTION!" Rauterkus shouted and the men stood at attention.

The captain stood in front of the vehicles and saluted when the colonel got out of the car.

"Good morning, Herr Oberst."

"Good morning, Hauptmann." Drechsler grinned broadly and embraced the captain. "Congratulations, Karl! Sabine called me. A boy!"

Rauterkus smiled proudly and fetched two small tin cylinders from the breast pocket of his uniform. "I brought them especially for this day."

"You should have brought more, Karl. Look who has come," Drechsler said, pointing to the US officers who had climbed out of the jeeps in the meantime.

The eyes of the lieutenant colonel with the face of an actor sparkled with pleasure. A cheerful looking sergeant major stood behind him.

"Your colonel has told us that you have become a father. I congratulate you, Captain Rauterkus," Frederick Miller said, reaching out his hand.

Rauterkus took the offered hand and squeezed it. His eyes were wet and he couldn't say a word.

Sergeant Major Clark was the next congratulant. "Congratulations, Captain. And all the best."

Rauterkus caught himself again and gave a short laugh. "Thank you, Sergeant Major."

He rummaged around in his breast pocket and found two more cigars. "I've packed them in reserve."

The four men faced each other, unscrewed the caps on the cylinders and took out the cigars. Happy laughter sounded over to the recruits, who watched in amazement as the four men patted each other on the shoulders, and looked very emotional.

"They seem to be good friends," one of the recruits whispered to his neighbor.

"And I thought they had fought each other in the war," the other returned from the corner of his mouth. "I guess they are really friends now."

Sergeant Voss seemed to have ears like a lynx, because he said with a knowing smile: "They are more than friends. They are brothers."

They were indeed. Brothers in arms.

Epilog

On December 16 the German Ardennes offensive began and the Battle of Hürtgen Forest came to a temporary end. Only after the final breakdown of the German offensive on January 10, 1945 the fighting in the Eifel was resumed.

On the German side all reserves were used up, the heavy losses could not be replaced. On February 8, Schmidt was finally taken over by the Americans.

Five months after the Allied troops had reached the Western border of the Hürtgen Forest, they stood on its Eastern side. On February 10, they conquered the dam of the Rur dam. By opening the dams, an artificial flood of the Rur was created, but this only delayed the American advance towards the Rhine by two weeks. The German resistance on the Western front quickly collapsed.

When US soldiers tell stories about the "eerie German forests", they are referring to their experiences in the Hürtgen Forest, one of the costliest battles in Western Europe.

The US Army lost about 33,000 men, of which 12,000 paid with their lives.

On the German side, it is assumed that about 28,000 men were lost, and also about 12,000 died.

This gives a picture of the intensity of the battles.

The fact that there are only two monuments is characteristic of the German approach to this battle. One of them is located on the cemetery of honor in Hürtgen; and both were erected by the former enemy, more precisely by the Veterans Association of the 22nd US Infantry Regiment.

The common care of wounded German and American soldiers really took place in this form and went down in history on the US side as the "Miracle of the Hürtgen Forest". The story of the "German Doctor" led to the fact that the doctor in charge at that time, Günther Stüttgen, was honored by the 28th Infantry Division of the US National Guard in 1996.

Hundreds of soldiers on both sides owed their lives to his actions. Stüttgen died in October 2003 in Berlin.

I would like to let Günther Stüttgen give the final words of this book:

"We had respect for each other. Respect that only soldiers who know the horror of war can have for each other."

THE END

History

The Huertgen Forest, located south of the Aachen-Düren line and west of the Rur, is today part of the North Eifel Nature Park. The area is accessible by numerous bicycle and hiking trails and leads through seemingly untouched nature. But not everywhere in the Eifel is this idyll to enjoy. Deviating from the marked paths can be very dangerous. Between October 1944 and February 1945, fierce fighting took place in the approximately 140 square kilometers of woodland, crisscrossed by narrow valleys and steep gorges, for which the term "massacre" is almost an understatement. These were the last defensive battles of the German Reich in the West, and the most loss-making of the US Army in a war zone. Even today, traces of the fighting can still be found. In many places, tank traps can be seen, there are also a handful of unexploded bunkers, and mines and unexploded ordnance still lurk in the ground, legacies of a war that dates back 75 years.

How did this battle, which is hardly known in Germany today, come about?

After the landing in Normandy, on June 6, 1944, the Western Allies fought their way through Northern France and pushed back the German troops. They had no other choice but to move towards the Benelux countries and establish a new line of defense there.

Due to the unexpectedly fast advance of the allied forces, the supply lines were overstretched and their offensive finally came to a standstill. In order to return to the war of movement, the Western Allies initiated Operation Market Garden, which took place between September 17 to September 27, 1944 in the Netherlands and the Lower Rhine. With the largest deployment of airborne troops in the history of mankind, important bridges were to be recaptured of the Germans and the advance was to be resumed. Although the front lines could be pushed forward as far as Belgium and the Netherlands in the course of the fighting, the airborne units suffered heavy losses due to the unexpectedly strong resistance of the Germans. The operation finally had to be abandoned.

Since then, the Allied High Command acted more cautiously. They had to realize that the Wehrmacht was by no means close to collapse ... that the victory over the Third Reich was not a foregone conclusion.

The Allies wanted to break through in a forest area near Hürtgen, between Aachen and Monschau, in order to flank the German units standing along the Rur front. If this succeeded, the way to the Rhine was open. For this reason, they attempted an attack through the Eifel mountain region without being aware of the terrain.

The American writer Ernest Hemingway witnessed the Battle of Hürtgen Forest as a war correspondent. Hemingway, who had previously glorified the war, later recounted his experiences in his novel "Across the River and into the Trees (1950)": "In Hürtgen the bodies just froze up hard, and it was so cold they froze up with ruddy faces...".

Most of the men who took part in this battle and survived it have died by now. Hardly anyone remembers their courage, their indescribable fear, their sacrifice and the fact that they were all soldiers in the service for their fatherland.

Glossary

Acht-Acht: German infamous 8.8 centimeter Flak anti-aircraft and anti-tank gun. Acht-Acht is German meaning nothing less than eight-eight.

Afrika Korps: German expeditionary force in North Africa; it was sent to Libya to support the Italian Armed Forces in 1941, since the Italians were not able to defend what they had conquered from the British and desperately needed some backing. Hitler's favorite general Rommel was the Afrika Korps' commander. Over the years he gained some remarkable victories over the British, but after two years of fierce fighting ... two years, in which the Axis' capabilities to move supplies and reinforcements over the Mediterranean Sea constantly decreased due to an allied air superiority that grew stronger by the day, Rommel no longer stood a chance against his opponents. Finally the U.S.A. entered the war and invaded North Africa in November 1942. Hitler prohibited the Afrika Korps to retreat back to Europe or even to shorten the front line by conducting tactical retreats. Because of that nearly 300 000 Axis' soldiers became POWs, with thousands of tons of important war supplies and weapons getting lost as well when the Afrika Korps surrendered in May 1943, just months after the 6th Army had surrendered in Stalingrad.

Assistant machine gunner: In the Wehrmacht you usually had three soldiers to handle one MG: a gunner and two assistants. The first assistant carried the spare barrel as well as some small tools for cleaning and maintaining the weapon plus extra belted ammunition in boxes. The second assistant carried even more ammunition around. In German the three guys are called: MG-1, MG-2 and MG-3.

Balkenkreuz: Well-known black cross on white background that has been used by every all-German armed force ever since and also before the first German unification by the Prussian military.

Close Combat Clasp: Award for participants in hand-to-hand fighting at close quarter. It was issued in bronze, silver and gold depending on the number of close combat fights the awarded soldier has taken part in

Comrade: This was a hard one for us. In the German military the term "Kamerad" is commonly used to address fellow soldiers, at the same time communists and social democrats call themselves "Genosse" in German. In English there only is this one word "comrade", and it often has a communistic touch. I guess an US-soldier would not call his fellow soldiers "comrade"? Since the word "Kamerad" is very, very common in the German military we decided to translate it with "comrade", but do not intend a communistic meaning in a German military context.

Danke: Thank you in German

EK 1: See Iron Cross

Faustpatrone ordnance device: See Knocker

Flak: German for AA-gun

Frau: Mrs.

Führer: Do I really have to lose any word about the most infamous German Austrian? (By the way, it is "Führer", not "Fuhrer". If you cannot find the "ü" on your keyboard, you can use "ue" as replacement).

Heeresgruppe: Army group. The Wehrmacht wasn't very consistent in naming their army groups. Sometime letters were used, sometimes names of locations or cardinal directions. To continue the madness high command frequently renamed their army groups. In this book "Heeresgruppe Mitte" refers to the center of the Eastern Front (= Army Group Center), "Heeresgruppe Süd" refers to the southern section (= Army Group South).

Heilige Mutter Maria: Old German exclamation, meaning "holy mother Mary", referring to Jesus' mother

Heimat: A less patriotic, more dreamy word than Vaterland (= fatherland) to address one's home country.

Herr: Mister (German soldiers address sex AND rank, meaning they would say "Mister sergeant" instead of "sergeant")

Herr General: In the German military, it does not matter which of the general ranks a general inhabits, he is always addressed by "Herr General". It is the same in the US military, I guess.

Hürtgenwald (Hürtgen Forest): A dense forest near the border to Belgium, at the same time the name refers to a municipality located within the Hürtgen Forest

Iron Cross: German war decoration restored by Hitler in 1939. It had been issued by Prussia during earlier military conflicts but in WW2 it was available to all German soldiers. There were three different tiers: Iron Cross (= Eisernes Kreuz) – 2nd class and 1st class –, Knight's Cross of the Iron Cross (= Ritterkreuz des Eisernen Kreuzes) – Knight's Cross without any features, Knight's Cross with Oak Leaves, Knight's Cross with Oak Leaves and Swords, Knight's Cross with Oak Leaves, Swords and Diamond and Knight's Cross with Golden Oak Leaves, Swords and Diamond –, and Grand Cross of the Iron Cross (= Großkreuz des Eisernen Kreuzes) – one without additional features and one called Star of the Grand Cross. By the way the German abbreviation for the Iron Cross 2nd class is EK2, alright?

Jawohl: A submissive substitute for "yes" (= "ja"), which is widely used in the German military, but also in daily life

K98k: Also Mauser 98k or Gewehr 98k (Gewehr = rifle). The K98k was the German standard infantry weapon during World War 2. The second k stands for "kurz", meaning it is a shorter version of the original rifle that already had been used in World War 1. Since it is a short version, it is correctly called carbine instead of rifle – the first k stands for "Karabiner", which is the German word for carbine.

Kampfgruppe: Combat formation that often was set up temporarily. Kampfgruppen had no defined size, some were of the size of a company, others were as big as a corps.

Kaputt: German word for "broken"; at one Point in the story Pappendorf uses this word describing a dead soldier. This means that he reduces the dead man to an object, since "kaputt" is only used for objects.

Knight's Cross: See Iron Cross

Knocker: German nickname for the Faustpatrone ordance device, the ancestor of the well-known Panzerfaust. German soldiers coined the nickname due to the bad penetrating power of this weapon. Often it just knocked at an enemy tank instead of penetrating its armor because its warhead simply bounced off instead of exploding.

Landser: German slang for a grunt

Luftwaffe: German Air Force

MG 42: German machine gun that features an incredible rate of fire of up to 1 500 rounds per minute (that's 25 per second!). It is also called "Hitler's buzzsaw", because a fire burst literally could cut someone in two halves. Its successor, the MG 3, is still in use in nowadays German Armed Forces (Bundeswehr).

MP40: German submachine gun, in service from 1938 to 1945

Panzerfaust: Single shot and cheap to produce German anti-tank weapon that was in service from 1943 to 1945. The weapon was distributed among poorly trained soldiers, Volkssturm men and Hitler Youth teenagers during the last months of the war in order to fight off enemy tank attacks.

Panzergrenadier: Motorized/mechanized infantry (don't mess with these guys!)

Panzerjäger I: First German tank destroyer. It featured an 4.7-centimeters gun. The name literally translates with "Tank Hunter 1".

Papa: Daddy

Scheisse: German for "Crap". Actually it is spelled "Scheiße" with an "ß", but since this letter is unknown in the English language and since it is pronounced very much like "ss", we altered it this way so that you do not mistake it for a "b".

Same thing holds true for the character Voss. In the original German text his name is written with an "ß", all through you also find Voss families in Germany with "ss" instead of "ß".

Sherman Tank (M4): Medium US-tank that was produced in very large numbers (nearly 50 000 were built between 1942 and 1945) and was used by most allied forces. Through the Lend-Lease program the tank also saw action on the Eastern Front. Its big advantage over all German panzers was its main gun stabilizer, which allowed for precise shooting while driving. German tankers were not allowed to shoot while driving due to Wehrmacht regulations. Because of the missing stabilizers it would have been a waste of ammunition anyway. The name of this US-tank refers to American Civil War general William Tecumseh Sherman.

Let's compare the dimensions: The Third Reich's overall tank production added up to around 50 000 between the pre-war phase and 1945 (all models and their variants like the 38 (t) Hetzer together, so: Panzer Is, IIs, IIIs, IVs, Panthers, Tigers, 38(t)s, Tiger IIs and Ferdinands/Elefants combined)!

Sir: Obviously Germans do not say "Sir", but that was the closest thing we could do to substitute a polite form that exists in the German language. There is no match for that in the English language: In German parts of a sentence changes when using the polite form. If one asks for a light in German, one would say "Hast du Feuer?" to a friend, but "Haben Sie Feuer?" to a stranger or any person one have not agreed with to leave away the polite form yet. During the Second World War the German polite form was commonly spread, in very conservative families children had to use the polite form to address their parents and even some couples used it among themselves. Today the polite form slowly is vanishing. Some companies like Ikea even addresses customers informally in the first place – something that was an absolute no-go 50 years ago.

In this one scene where the Colonel argues with First Lieutenant Haus he gets upset, because Haus does not say "Sir" (once more: difficult to translate). In the Wehrmacht a superior was addressed with "Herr" plus his rank, in the Waffen SS the "Herr" was left out; a soldier was addressed only by his rank like it is common in armed forces of English-speaking countries. Also one would leave the "Herr" out when one wants to disparage the one addressed, like Papendorf often does when calling Berning "Unteroffizier" instead of "Herr Unteroffizier".

Stahlhelm: German helmet with its distinctive coal scuttle shape, as Wikipedia puts it. The literal translation would be steel helmet.

Vaterland: Fatherland

Willkommen: German word for welcome

Wound Badge: German decoration for wounded soldiers or those, who suffered frostbites. The wound badge was awarded in three stages: black for being wounded once or twice, silver for the third and fourth wound, gold thereafter. US equivalent: Purple Heart.

Wehrmacht Ranks (Army)

All military branches have their own ranks, even the medical service.

Rank	US equivalent
Anwärter	Candidate (NCO or officer)
Soldat (or Schütze, Kanonier, Pionier, Funker, Reiter, Jäger, Grenadier ... depends on the branch of service)	Private
Obersoldat (Oberschütze, Oberkanonier ...)	Private First Class
Gefreiter	Lance Corporal
Obergefreiter	Senior Lance Corporal
Stabsgefreiter	Corporal
Unteroffizier	Sergeant
Fahnenjunker	Ensign
Unterfeldwebel/Unterwachtmeister (Wachtmeister only in cavalry and artillery)	Staff Sergeant
Feldwebel/Wachtmeister	Master Sergeant
Oberfeldwebel/Oberwachtmeister	Master Sergeant
Oberfähnrich	Ensign First Class
Stabsfeldwebel/Stabswachtmeister	Sergeant Major
Hauptfeldwebel	This is not a rank, but an NCO function responsible for personnel and order within a company
Leutnant	2nd Lieutenant
Oberleutnant	1st Lieutenant

Hauptmann/Rittmeister (Rittmeister only in cavalry and artillery)	Captain
Major	Major
Oberstleutnant	Lieutenant Colonel
Oberst	Colonel
Generalmajor	Major General
Generalleutnant	Lieutenant General
General der ... (depends on the branch of service: Infanterie (Infantry) Kavallerie (Cavalry) Artillerie (Artillery) Panzertruppe (Tank troops) Pioniere (Engineers) Gebirgstruppe (Mountain Troops) Nachrichtentruppe (Signal Troops)	General (four-star)
Generaloberst	Colonel General
Generalfeldmarschall	Field Marshal

About the Author

Stefan Köhler was a KFOR and ISAF veteran in Afghanistan in combat operations and was wounded there. Nobody can put the horrors of war on paper as relentlessly as someone who has experienced them first-hand. Stefan Köhler writes to the point, his texts never let go of the reader.

Your Satisfaction Is Our Goal!

Dear Reader,

We hope you enjoyed this book. Do you have any comments, criticism or ideas for books you want to read in the future? Please do not hesitate to contact us. We read every Email personally and answer it as soon as possible. Your opinion is of great value for us.

Contact us: info@ek2-publishing.com

You can help us to keep history alive by taking a moment's time to review this book on Amazon. Many positive reviews lead to more visibility for our books. A few words or a simple star review help our authors and our publishing company to increase our quality with every book published. Thank you for your support!

PS: In rare case scenarios a book might get damaged during shipment. If that should be the case, please do not hesitate to contact us and we will replace the book at no charge.

Your EK-2 Publishing Team
The publisher close to its readers

Our recommendations for you!

Iron Cross – Never Surrender!
Book 1
By Tom Zola

In November 1942, Hitler dies in a plane crash. The Nazi Party collapses, and the German military takes over. Facing defeat, they launch a last-ditch panzer offensive at Kursk to stop the advancing Soviets.

Shingas
By Barry Cole

»Shingas« tells the tragic tale of the fight between the Iroquois tribe and the overpowering British troops. Especially the warrior Shingas battles them with merciless brutality. Experience the conquest of the American East through the eyes of this fearless warrior.

Available on all major platforms!

Published by EK-2 Publishing GmbH

Friedensstraße 12
47228 Duisburg - Germany
Register court: Duisburg - Germany
Company registration number: HRB 30321
CEO: Monika Münstermann

E-Mail: info@ek2-publishing.com
Website: www.ek2-publishing.com

Cover art: Mario Heyer
Author: Stefan Köhler
Translation: Martina Wehr
Editing: Jill Marc Münstermann
Layout: Eduard Krisan

1. edition, April 2025

Made in United States
Cleveland, OH
09 May 2025

16797887R00059